AF521999

# SUNDAY KIND OF LOVE

## Lois Faye Dyer

A KISMET™ Romance

METEOR PUBLISHING CORPORATION

Bensalem, Pennsylvania

KISMET™ is a trademark of Meteor Publishing Corporation



First Printing December 1991.

ISBN: 1-878702-70-X



Printed in the United States of America

For my Mother,
whose shining example taught her six children,
what it means to be a woman of substance, dignity, honor and courage.

## LOIS FAYE DYER

Winner of the 1989–1990 Romantic Times Reviewer's Choice Award for Best New Series Author, Lois Faye Dyer lives on Washington State's beautiful Puget Sound with her husband, two children, and their irascible parrot, Dylan. She ended a career as a paralegal and Superior Court Clerk to fulfill a life-long dream to write and when she's not involved in writing, she enjoys long walks on the beach with her husband, watching musical and western movies from the 1940's and 1950's and, most of all, indulging her passionate addiction to reading.

**Other KISMET books by Lois Faye Dyer:**

No. 4 *WINTERFIRE*
No. 21 *THAT JAMES BOY*

# ONE

Sunday afternoon in CastleRock, Iowa, was perfect for jogging. Not too hot, not too chilly. The late-September sun lacked the burning heat of summer, but its mellow golden light was the perfect accompaniment to the scent of burning leaves drifting on the autumn air.

Lily Townsend loved running. Not only did the exercise leave her feeling exhilarated, but she welcomed the uninterrupted time spent with just her thoughts. She breathed deeply, dragging in the faintly acrid scent of burning leaves.

*I love it here,* she thought to herself, a smile of pure pleasure and contentment curving her mouth. *For the first time in five years, I feel safe!*

She jogged easily through an older section of CastleRock. Here, the large two-story, turn-of-the-century homes were set back from the broad street in the centers of wide green lawns. The crisp autumn nights had turned the towering oaks and maples into a glory of red and gold that dotted the lawns and lined the streets. Their colorful leaves drifted earthward—littering lawns, driveways, and sidewalks alike with a spattering of brilliant color that crunched and crackled beneath her feet.

The city sidewalks in this older section of town were uneven in places, and Lily's quick glance inspected the strip of concrete squares ahead of her. In several spots, tree roots had wedged their way beneath the paved blocks, shoving them upward and slanting them several inches above their neighbors.

Eyes on the ground, she jogged onward. This was her third mile and perspiration dotted her upper lip and dampened her scalp beneath sun-warmed ebony hair. Caught into a pony tail high on her head and braided, the glossy black swath of silk swung back and forth as she ran, her bare brown legs pumping rhythmically. Thick black lashes narrowed over eyes that were a startlingly clear violet in the tanned oval of her face. Her eyes weren't the only unusual feature in a finely molded face that boasted a short, patrician nose, high cheekbones, a mouth with a lushly full lower lip and perfectly bowed upper curve, and a determined little chin. Black brows winged above the thickly lashed lavender eyes. The white cotton T-shirt she wore had ''Rolling Stones—Steel Wheels Tour'' printed across her chest, and navy shorts left the long length of her curvy legs bare above white tennis socks and running shoes.

Los Angeles and the nightmare of the last five years seemed a million miles away from CastleRock, Iowa, and her new job as director for the small town's junior symphony. The position was split between the symphony and the local high school, where she taught classes in music. Already, there were several young students who delighted her musician's heart.

But even more importantly, she was making friends. Meg Stewart, mother of one of her more talented students, had taken Lily under her wing. It was Meg who had introduced her to Sarah McFadden and the two had quickly become fast friends. For Lily, whose growing up years as a child musical prodigy had been spent with tutors and adults in a restricted, rarified atmosphere, having women friends was a delightful, welcome experience.

She ran lightly past the Campbells' house and lifted a hand in answer to ten-year-old Michael's shouted greeting. Over the last two months, Lily had often stopped to chat with Mike, but today she was short of time. Michael was content with a wave, but his Dalmatian puppy was not. Ears flopping and tail wagging, he left the pile of leaves he was rooting his wet black nose into and gamboled across the lawn to the sidewalk.

"Go home, Hobbes." Lily tried her best to sound stern, but couldn't help laughing as his expressive face went from puppy-dog joy to woebegone despair at her refusal to stop and play.

The Campbells' house was on a corner lot, and tall hedges edged the far side, making it impossible to see oncoming traffic. Distracted by the puppy, Lily shot a quick glance up and down the street, thought it empty, and stepped off the curb. From the corner of her vision, she caught a blur of moving orange and realized, too late, that a car was almost on top of her.

The powerful orange Camaro rumbled throatily as Trace McFadden downshifted. Preoccupied with thoughts of a cranky engine in the '36 Ford he'd just spent the afternoon working on in his shop, he didn't notice the jogger until it was too late.

The front end of the Camaro was well into the turn onto Webster Avenue when the woman stepped off the curb and directly into its path.

"Damn—!" Trace swore in shock, and hit the brakes.

But it was too late. Even though the heavy car was only

moving at fifteen to twenty miles per hour, still, the slender woman was no match for the thirty-eight-hundred-pound machine. Trace caught only the flash of white shirt and the pale, shocked blur of her face before she was knocked off her feet and disappeared beyond the car's front fender.

"Oh, my God!"

He twisted the key to kill the engine and the car was still rocking from the sudden, abrupt stop when he shoved open the door and jumped out to race around the hood of the Camaro. Sprawled on the pavement a scant three feet from the right front tire was the jogger.

Trace dropped down beside her and froze, halted as surely and abruptly as if he'd walked into a brick wall. The woman lying on the pavement was the most impossibly beautiful female he'd ever seen. His stunned gaze took in a long braid of ebony hair falling over one shoulder, the loose, unbraided end curling against bare skin where the boat neckline of a white T-shirt was ripped. Her body was lushly, extravagantly curved, the long brown legs marred with angry red scratches below blue shorts. Thick black lashes lay in sooty crescents against fragile skin.

With an effort, he forced his numb muscles to move, and his fingers overlapped around her slender wrist. He lifted it gently, searching for and finding the steady pulse that throbbed beneath soft skin. His broad chest expanded in a deep sigh of relief.

"Jeez, Trace!" Mike Campbell skidded to a stop at Trace's shoulder and he peered down at Lily. His brown eyes were wide with fear, the orangey-brown dots of his freckles standing out in relief against his white face. "Is she dead?"

"No, Mike," Trace answered, his worried gaze fastened on her pale face. "But I don't know how badly she's hurt. We need an ambulance. Go ask your mom to call one, okay?''

''Sure.'' He took off in a flash of freckles, tennis shoes, and blue jeans.

''Hey, Mike!'' Trace yelled, and the ten-year-old skidded to a stop to look back at him.

''Yeah?''

''Tell them to hurry!''

''Right, Trace!'' The sturdy boy spun around and sprinted across the lawn and up the steps of his house, the door slamming loudly behind him.

Trace turned his attention back to the woman. The hem of her white T-shirt had been pulled up her body when she slid across the pavement, baring the silky skin of her midriff and the pale ecru satin and lace of her bra. The shirt was stained with dirt and traces of blood from the angry red scratches that marred the soft, exposed skin.

He smoothed the stained shirt down over her midriff, trying unsuccessfully to ignore the lure of silky skin and warm woman beneath the satin bra when his knuckles grazed the underside of her breast. She stirred beneath his hand and he yanked his fingers away from the hem of her shirt and glanced quickly up at her face.

The thick fringe of black lashes lifted slowly, revealing huge violet eyes, glazed with pain and misted with tears. They shone like lavender jewels in the pale oval of her face and fastened on Trace's face with stunned intensity.

Lily opened her eyes and looked up to find a blond giant bending anxiously over her. For a moment, she forgot the pain and simply stared at him. He was heartstoppingly handsome, with high cheekbones, straight nose, sensual mouth, and dark brows. A twisted blue handkerchief was tied around his forehead to keep shaggy blond hair out of his eyes—eyes that were so deep a blue that they gleamed like brilliant blue sapphires in his tanned face. A ragged gray sweatshirt covered his broad chest, the cut-off sleeves baring teak-brown arms sculpted with muscles. Faded, ripped jeans covered heavily muscled thighs and long legs ending in lace-up worn black workboots. Lily thought hazily that he looked like a Viking warrior—but that was ridiculous. What would a Viking be doing in CastleRock, Iowa?

The Viking smoothed a strand of hair away from her cheek with gentle, calloused fingers. Lily fought down a shiver of awareness.

"How do you feel?" His deep voice rumbled, husky with concern, and the sound shook Lily from her absorbed study of him.

Trace was worried. She was staring at him with unblinking intensity and a faint, other-world expression on her lovely, pale face.

The sound of his voice wiped out the insulating absorption, and in its place, Lily instantly became aware that every bone in her body hurt. The lush curve of her mouth was vulnerable as she fought to keep from whimpering. It was a battle she lost as she struggled to sit up, a moan escaping from lips that trembled despite her efforts.

"Lie still," Trace ordered, his voice rough with the panic that surged in his throat. "You might have broken something! Where does it hurt?"

"Everywhere," Lily managed to get out, grateful for the hard hands that eased her back to the pavement.

Trace had to bend close to hear the husky murmur. His nostrils flared, inhaling a scent that was a mixture of musky Oriental perfume and heated woman. His body responded with an immediate, physical stirring.

Lily saw the flare of blue fire in the depths of his eyes, but before her pain-hazed senses could register its meaning, the flame was gone, replaced by worried concern. He sat up and ripped his sweatshirt off over his head, baring a broad chest rippling with sleek muscles.

Gentle hands lifted her and tucked the rolled up sweatshirt beneath her head.

"Did you hurt your head when you fell?" he asked, letting his fingers move slowly, testingly, over her scalp, determinedly ignoring the seductive slide of silky black hair beneath his fingers.

"Yes," she murmured hazily, closing her eyes.

"Yeah," he muttered to himself, frowning as his questing fingers discovered an egg-size lump behind her ear. "You sure did."

He slid his hands away from her and felt a moment of panic when he realized that a bright smear of blood stained his fingers. He caught her chin and gently tilted her face toward him, finding with relief that the blood came from a shallow scratch just above the hairline behind her ear.

"I don't think you broke anything," he murmured to himself, running his hands lightly over her legs and arms, struggling to remain unaffected and failing miserably.

Lily opened her eyes at his words. His head was bent as he carefully inspected an angry abrasion on her left elbow. A shock of wheat-blond hair fell over the blue bandanna, the dark brows drawn down in a V as he frowned in concentration. He glanced up, sapphire eyes meeting her own lavender ones with an impact that was staggering.

"I'm so damn sorry," he said, his deep voice rasping over a throat gone dry with emotion. "I didn't even see you until it was too late."

"It wasn't your fault," Lily said softly, deeply affected by the genuine anguish she saw in the depths of his blue eyes. "I wasn't paying attention." She smiled, a sweet, forgiving curve of her lips.

And Trace fell in love. Just that simply. Just that

quickly. He actually felt his heart expand, take wings and leave his body.

Lily stared up at him, snared by the fierce, intense blue stare and the stunned, absolute stillness that gripped his big body. One hand cradled her arm, the fingers curled possessively around her bicep while the fingers of his other hand stroked compulsively, warmly over the soft skin on the inside of her elbow.

Trace wanted badly to fold her into his arms, to kiss that soft mouth and whisper again how sorry he was for hurting her and promise her that nothing would ever hurt her again. But before he could, the scream of a siren split the afternoon air at the exact moment that Mike skidded to a stop behind him.

"The ambulance is on its way, Trace," he said breathlessly. "Mom said not to get in your way. She would have come out, but she still can't walk very well with those darn crutches. She said I was to ask you if there's anything she can do," he added, staring with worried eyes at the blood welling from the scratches on Lily's bare legs.

"Thanks, Mike." With a giant effort of will, Trace forced his gaze away from Lily. He smiled at the boy's pale, freckled face and ruffled the shock of brown hair with a big hand. For the first time, he realized that a crowd of neighborhood residents stood in a half-circle behind him, watching with worried concern and murmuring to each other. "You did everything we needed."

Mike's chest expanded with pride and he grinned back at the broad-shouldered man.

"Here's the ambulance," someone in the crowd called. Trace and Mike looked up just in time to see the vehicle turning the corner onto their block.

"Thank God!" Trace breathed in relief. He looked down at Lily and smoothed a strand of ebony silk from her cheek. "The ambulance is nearly here, honey," he said soothingly, not noticing the endearment that slipped out as naturally as if he'd known her for years. Lily didn't seem to notice, either, her dark lashes lifted briefly, lavender gaze meeting blue before they fell again.

The ambulance siren split the silence of the quiet neighborhood and brought more residents out of their houses. By the time the uniformed attendants reached Trace and Lily, the crowd of concerned onlookers had swollen to nearly two dozen.

"What happened, Trace?" The ambulance attendants nodded a brief hello as they knelt to examine Lily.

"I hit her," he said bleakly, watching with dread as they checked her reflexes. Kelly's dark gaze left his patient and flicked quickly up to meet Trace's blue stare, one black brow lifting questioningly. "With the car, Kelly, not my fist!"

The black-haired EMT nodded briefly and turned back to Lily.

"Is she going to be all right?" Trace demanded, anxiety threading his deep tones.

"Don't know yet," Kelly responded, his gaze fastened on his patient. "My guess would be yes—probably—but we won't really know for sure until we get her to the hospital and the doctors check her out."

Trace hovered, hating the feeling of helplessness that gripped him when he had to stand aside and watch the two men carefully strap Lily onto a gurney. He wanted to join her in the ambulance, but at the last minute, decided to follow the emergency vehicle in his own car.

Fortunately for Trace, the local police were busy elsewhere or he would surely have gotten a speeding ticket. Sirens wailing and lights flashing, the ambulance raced across town. Trace followed it like a shadow, running red lights and stop signs with a fine disregard for the law. As a result, he arrived at the hospital practically on its bumper, and by the time the technicians lowered the gurney to the sidewalk, Trace was beside them.

The nurse wouldn't let him follow Lily into the curtained-off examination room so he paced the confines of the waiting room until a white-coated doctor pushed through the swinging doors.

"Alex . . ." Trace walked swiftly across the gleaming waxed tile. "How is she?"

"She's going to be fine, Trace," Dr. Kingston said soothingly. "Just fine."

"Thank God," Trace muttered with heartfelt relief. "When I saw her lying there on the street—"

"Exactly how did it happen?"

"I was on my way home from the shop. I'd just turned onto Webster Avenue when she ran off the curb and right into me, and the front right bumper of the Camaro knocked her down. It happened so fast, I couldn't stop before I hit her. You're sure she's going to be all right?"

"Yes, I'm sure." Alex thrust his hands into the deep pockets of the lab coat he wore and stared at Trace with curious speculation. He'd known Trace for years—they'd gone to grade school and high school together—and he couldn't remember ever seeing him this upset before. "She's got a few contusions, some abrasions, a bruised rib, and a nasty knot on her head, but nothing life threatening. I'm going to keep her in the hospital overnight for observation, but unless something unforeseen develops, I'm sure she'll be able to go home in the morning."

Trace's chest lifted and fell in a huge sigh, the deep-seated fear that tortured him giving way to relief.

"Thank God! Can I see her?"

"Sure, I don't see why not. The nurse should have her settled into her room—third floor, east wing. She might be asleep by now, though. I prescribed a sedative and a painkiller that at the very least will have her groggy. Don't be surprised if she has trouble following a conversation—that medication packs quite a punch."

"Thanks, Alex." Trace turned and strode away several steps before he halted abruptly and walked back to Alex. "Uh, Alex?"

"Yes?" Alex looked up from the assignment list for emergency-room personnel he was reading.

"There's one other thing. Who is she?"

Alex stared at Trace for a startled moment before a broad grin creased his handsome face.

"Who is she? You mean you don't know?"

"No, I don't know. And what's so damn funny?" Trace asked testily.

"What's funny is that you, of all people, don't know who she is. She's probably the most beautiful unmarried female in CastleRock. I thought you had radar that automatically picked up on every eligible woman within a hundred miles!" He laughed uproariously and Trace glared at him.

"Yeah? Well, you thought wrong," he growled. "Stop laughing like a hyena and tell me who she is."

"Of course, she isn't a blonde," Alex went on, somehow managing to get words out between chuckles. "And everybody knows you specialize in blondes."

"Funny, Alex, real funny. Now suppose you stop laughing and just tell me her name."

"All right, all right," Alex managed to stop laughing long enough to tell him. "It's Lily, Lily Townsend."

"Lily," Trace repeated to himself, liking the sound of it. It fit his beautiful brunette, with her long, elegant legs, curvy body, and vibrant coloring.

Alex said something else, but Trace didn't hear him. He was already striding away, heading for the elevator that would take him to the third floor and Lily. Alex shook his head in amusement and turned back to his list.

"Room 322—322 . . ." Trace murmured to himself as he walked down the wide hallway, scanning the doors and their numbers. The nurse at the station down the hall behind him leaned out over the counter to stare with appreciation at his backside in faded tight jeans as he walked away from her, but for once, he was completely oblivious to female interest.

He pushed open the door to Room 322 and stepped inside, his gaze quickly scanning the two-bed room and finding one of the beds empty. Sunlight poured through the half-closed blinds and into the room, making a pattern of gold-and-black bars on the polished white floor between the two beds. Trace walked quietly across the sun-drenched tiles to the bed and stood silently, looking down at Lily. Her hair was still in a braid, but tendrils had escaped to curl in wisps of black silk around her face. Thick black lashes lay in dark crescents against pale skin, her lips a soft, pale pink in her wan face. The torn T-shirt had been replaced by a short-sleeved white hospital gown, and the bed sheet was tucked beneath her bare arms, her hands lying palms-up at her sides, slim fingers curling slightly inward. Her body seemed smaller, enfolded as it was in the sterile efficiency of hospital garb and bedding.

Trace reached out a forefinger and gently traced the soft skin of her arm where a long scratch was painted with orange-colored antiseptic. He was fighting a wave of raw emotion when those dark lashes lifted and she looked up at him. The lavender eyes stared solemnly at him, the dark pupils dilated and nearly engulfing the violet ring surrounding them.

"Hi," he said softly, his deep voice husky as he forced it past a throat gone tight with emotion.

Lily blinked, staring up at the tall Viking bending over her. He was holding her arm and his fingers were pleasantly rough where they smoothed rhythmically over the skin of her forearm.

"This is a wonderful dream," she said hazily, accepting the floaty, out-of-body feeling that engulfed her. "I like Vikings. Where's your dragon ship?"

Trace stared at her, confused, until he remembered Alex's warning about the medication he'd given her. *A Viking?* he thought to himself, an amused grin tilting his mouth. *That must have been one hell of a painkiller they gave you, honey!*

"I left it at the dock," he said, straight-faced.

"Oh." She nodded with complete acceptance. "I'm sure you're a great hero, but I've already been rescued." She yawned delicately, lashes drooping over her eyes. "You can kiss me, though, before I go to sleep."

"Kiss you?" Nonplussed, Trace stared at her, trying to ignore the way his heart surged and beat faster at her words. "You want me to kiss you?"

"Of course." Her eyes widened, a little frown creasing a V between the arched brows.

Trace shrugged mentally. *Oh, well,* he thought philosophically. *It's your dream, sweetheart. Far be it from me to object!*

He bent over the bed and brushed a chaste kiss against the soft skin of her temple, nostrils flaring as he drew in the elusive smell of her perfume. He straightened and looked down at her only to find her frowning at him in obvious disapproval, censure apparent in the lavender depths of her eyes.

"What?" he asked.

"That's not the way the hero is supposed to kiss the heroine," she complained, wrinkling her nose in disgust.

"No?" Trace grinned, wondering if she would remember all this when she woke up tomorrow.

"No." She shook her head emphatically, wincing as

the movement tugged her hair against the swollen place behind her ear. "Come here," she whispered, and crooked a finger at him.

Trace bent toward her, obeying that commanding finger and wondering what it was that she wanted to whisper to him.

Lily slid her arms around the Viking's neck and tugged him closer, lifting her mouth to his. His lips were warm and surprisingly soft, his breath sweet when he breathed a startled gasp against her mouth. She sighed with contentment and nuzzled closer. He smelled like wind and sunshine, underlaid with the clean scent of soap and the faint, not unpleasant flavor of machine oil.

After that first startled second when his lips lay still above hers, her Viking came alive. His arms slid under and around her and half-lifted her off the bed to cradle her gently against a satisfyingly solid male chest while he explored the shape of her mouth with his. The hospital room faded away, the world narrowing to hold only the two of them and the heat generated by the long, slow pressure of his lips moving against hers. By the time his mouth lifted from hers, they were both breathless, hearts shuddering against rib cages.

Lily lifted drowsy lashes to look up at him, her arms sliding from around his neck, one hand lingering to push a strand of blond hair off his brow and trace the bones of his cheek and jaw before falling limply to rest against the white sheet. Arousal flushed his face and glittered in the depths of eyes gone dark with need.

"See," Lily said, her voice husky with her own stirred emotions. "*That's* how you're supposed to kiss." She turned on her side and snuggled into the pillow. "Remember that next time," she said sleepily, her lashes dropping closed as she gave in to the lure of the medication and drifted into sleep.

Trace drew a deep breath, his arms braced on the mattress and bracketing the soft curves of her body while his chest lifted and fell in a labored effort. When she turned on her side toward him, she curled her legs, and her thighs snugged against his hip, her body warmth seeping through the sheet and his jeans. He felt surrounded by her and he wanted nothing more than to climb beneath the sheets and hold her against him. He'd felt desire and lust before, but this urge to hold, cherish, and protect a woman was completely new.

He watched Lily sleeping for long moments before he reluctantly slid off the bed and stood up. He didn't remember sitting down on the edge of the bed, but then, he doubted that he would have been able to remember his name when his lavender-eyed seductress pulled him down and kissed him.

He bent and brushed a chaste kiss against her brow, breathing in the scent of her perfume almost buried beneath the faintly astringent smell of hospital soap and antiseptic.

"I promise I'll remember next time," he whispered softly to the sleeping woman. He stood watching her for a few more moments before reluctantly leaving the room. He didn't even notice the come-hither smile of a nurse who passed him in the hall as he drifted dazedly out of the hospital.

# TWO

Trace looked vastly different the following morning when Nurse Adams stopped him in the third-floor hallway. Gone was the sleeveless sweatshirt, worn jeans, and scuffed work boots. Instead, a pale-blue, button-up-the-front cotton dress shirt covered his broad shoulders, the tails tucked into black slacks neatly belted with black leather. Polished black loafers covered his feet. Gone also was the makeshift blue bandanna sweatband. Instead, his wheat-blond hair was side-parted, brushed behind his ears, and combed neatly, curling against his collar at his nape. A gold watchband circled his wrist below folded-back shirt cuffs and bare forearms.

"No, Trace," Nurse Adams said firmly. "Visiting hours aren't until two o'clock. You'll have to come back this afternoon."

"I can't, Mary. Alex told me that she'll be released this morning. If you won't let me see her now, I'll miss her entirely. Come on," he coaxed. "Please."

Mary Adams was sixty-three years old and the grandmother of six, but she wasn't immune to the powerful appeal of Trace McFadden at his most charming. She smiled wryly and gave in.

"All right, all right," she said. "But mind you, no more than ten minutes!" she called after his retreating back.

Trace tossed her an acquiescent grin and strode down the hall to push open the door to Room 322.

Lily looked up expectantly as the door swung open. Nurse Adams had told her earlier that her doctor would be making his rounds within the hour and if he agreed, she would be released. Anxious to leave the comfort of the hospital room that she couldn't possibly afford, she ignored the twinges from her bruises and pinned a smile on her face, but the man who stepped into the room wasn't wearing a lab coat and she'd never seen anyone who looked less like a doctor. Tanned, broad-shouldered, with the blondest hair and bluest eyes she'd ever seen, he paused just inside the door and looked at her. Her hands stilled and she forgot to pull the brush through her hair, mesmerized by the sapphire gaze that inspected her, moving over her features with an almost physical touch.

Trace momentarily lost his voice and forgot how to speak. Lily was sitting up in bed, propped against pillows, and her long mane of ebony hair fell around her shoulders in a gleaming black cape of silk. A dark bruise marred the pale skin of one cheek and the lavender eyes were shadowed. As he watched, the small smile that tilted her lips faded, and a tiny frown drew down the delicate arch of her brows.

"You're not the doctor," she said. Trace knew the moment she realized who he was because the confusion left her face and the violet eyes grew cool. He waited, but she just sat there, calmly watching him with a remote, reserved lavender gaze.

"No, I'm not the doctor." He approached the bed but

stopped at the foot. The cool-eyed woman watching him wasn't the same woman who had pulled him down and kissed him with such enthusiasm the night before. Where had she gone and how deeply beneath the wall of cool reserve had this Lily buried that other, vulnerable, passionate woman? "I was driving the car that hit you. My name is Trace, Trace McFadden."

Lily already knew he was the rugged Viking that had been driving the orange car that hit her. There was something else about him, something that nagged at the edge of her memory, something that she should remember, but his words drove everything else from her mind. No expression flitted across her still face, but his name sent shock waves reverberating through her body beneath its cool outer shell. *Trace McFadden!* This was Sarah's adored older brother. This was also the CastleRock ladykiller whose reputation had reached Lily's ears before she'd been in town a week.

And much to Lily's dismay, this was also the man who was causing her heart to beat faster and a warm, breathless anticipation to inhibit her breathing. She'd thought she was immune to sexy, charming males. She hadn't felt the slightest twinge of interest in more than five years.

*Oh, no, why now? And why him—anybody but him!*

But none of her emotions showed on her face; there was only a faint wariness reflected in her eyes. She drew on her many years of stage experience and hid her emotions behind a faint smile.

"It's kind of you to stop by, Mr. McFadden, but as you can see, the only damage was a few bumps and bruises."

"Thank God." Trace smiled in relief. "No ill effects from the bump on the head?"

Lily's fingers flew involuntarily to the bump behind her ear, greatly deflated but still tender beneath her touch.

"I don't think so—just a little headache."

"Good. You scared me to death when you stepped off that curb in front of me. Didn't you see my car?"

"No. I was jogging by the Campbell house and Michael's puppy ran across the lawn. I remember telling him to go home and I suppose he must have distracted me just long enough for me to miss seeing you. I only remember catching a glimpse of orange before I was hit."

Trace winced, sapphire eyes scanning her pale face.

"I'm so damn sorry. I can't tell you how sorry I am. I didn't even see you. One minute I was turning onto Webster Avenue and the next second you were right in front of the car."

Lily was surprised at the depth of anguish apparent on his face and in his voice.

"It wasn't your fault. I should have been paying closer attention." Anxious to change the subject, Lily gestured at the sheaf of flowers in his hand, half hidden in a cone of florist's green waxed paper. "Are those for me?"

"Yes, they are," Trace lifted the forgotten flowers and stepped closer to the bed to lay them in her arms. She bent her head to them and closed her eyes, thick lashes making ebony fans against her skin as she inhaled the fragrance of red roses.

"Thank you." She glanced up at him, her eyes glowing with violet light beneath the screen of black lashes. "They're lovely."

*Not half as lovely as you,* he wanted to say.

"Are you being released today?" he asked instead.

"I hope so," she sighed and glanced worriedly at the closed hall door. "I won't know until the doctor makes his rounds."

"If he releases you, I'd be glad to give you a ride home," Trace said casually, shoving his hands into his slacks pockets to keep them from reaching out to smooth the little worried frown lines from between her brows.

"No, thank you," she answered, softly but firmly.

"It's the least I can do, since it's my fault you're here in the first place," he said, smiling slowly at her.

Lily determinedly ignored the warm curl of heat in her midsection.

"Thank you, but no. And I'm not so sure it's your fault I'm in this hospital bed; I strongly suspect it was mostly my own fault."

"I can't say I agree with you about that, but if you're sure—"

"I'm sure," Lily interrupted, her soft voice leaving no doubt that she wouldn't change her mind.

"Well, I—"

The hall door pushed inward decisively and Alex's voice interrupted Trace.

"Good morning, Miss Townsend. And Trace . . ." He grinned at his friend, knowing full well that Trace didn't appreciate the interruption. "What are you doing here so early on a Monday morning? Who's watching the shop?"

Half-turned away from Lily to face the door, Trace threw Alex a threatening glare.

"Charlie and George are both at the shop." He had to bite his tongue to keep from snarling at Alex's knowing grin. "And I stopped by to see how Miss Townsend was doing."

"How nice of you," Alex said, tongue in cheek, "but I'm afraid I'll have to ask you to cut your visit short so I can examine Miss Townsend."

Trace's blue gaze promised retribution, but it gentled as he turned back to Lily.

"Thank you for the flowers, Mr. McFadden, and for stopping by. I appreciate your concern."

She was politely dismissing him. Trace knew it, and his wry smile told her he understood exactly what she was doing. It also told her that he was going to let her get away with it, for now.

"I'm glad you're feeling better, Miss Townsend," he said politely. "I won't say good-bye since I'm sure we'll be running into each other. Often. CastleRock is a small town." His cheeks creased in a heartstopping grin, those sapphire eyes gleaming warmly, and then he was gone, the hospital door swishing quietly shut behind him.

Lily lifted the roses to her cheek, their cool, fragrant petals soft against her skin. She stared unseeingly at the closed door. She couldn't afford to feel this way about a man. There would never be a future for her with another man, and no room for love in her life. Not even the temporary kind that gossip said Trace McFadden specialized in. She only hoped that he had gotten the message that she wasn't interested in dalliance, but remembering the warm promise in those blue eyes, she had the uneasy feeling that she hadn't seen the last of Sarah's big brother.

Trace sprawled in a comfortable stuffed chair in his dad's den, his long legs stretched out in front of him, his scuffed tennis shoes propped on a hassock, and scowled unseeingly at the television screen.

"Touchdown!" Gavin's delighted roar broke into his preoccupation, and he focused on the big color screen. Iowa University's Hawkeyes had just scored and Gavin was on his feet, yelling with excitement.

Trace managed to mumble an appropriate response and sank back into preoccupation as the teams regrouped.

*Damn it!* he thought with frustration. *If I only played a musical instrument I could join the symphony—except I'm too old for the Junior Symphony.*

He'd been wracking his brain all week, and after exhausting all of his extensive resources, had gotten little or no information about Lily Townsend. The grapevine told him that she was undoubtedly beautiful, unquestionably wonderful at her job, and completely inaccessible. The lady went to work and went home. Period. She didn't date; she didn't frequent any of the town's local spots where single, unmarried people gathered, and so far, had exhibited no interest in any group pursuits. Other than jogging, which she evidently had to give up until her bruises healed, he couldn't find one single opportunity to waylay her by "accident." He was stymied. Stalemated. And he didn't like it. Not one single bit.

He mumbled an excuse to his dad and ambled down the hall to the kitchen. He was standing with his head in the refrigerator, frowning distractedly, when his sister walked into the room.

Sarah propped her shoulder against the door frame, crossed her arms, and watched her brother while he alternately frowned and sighed into the depths of the refrigerator.

"What in heaven's name are you doing?" she asked with curiosity.

Startled, Trace swung around and, in doing so, cracked his elbow on the fridge door.

"Ouch," he growled, rubbing his aching elbow. "Not that it's any of your business, but I'm making a sandwich."

"Aaaaah." Sarah nodded her head wisely and lifted a brow at the assortment of food sitting atop the butcher block table in the center of the room. "Since when did you start putting yogurt on your sandwiches?"

Trace looked at the tabletop and felt a flush move up his cheeks. He picked up the carton of strawberry yogurt and put it back on the refrigerator shelf before collecting a bunch of radishes and replacing them in the vegetable crisper.

"You seem to have something on your mind." Sarah took a seat at the table, propped her elbows on the scrubbed wood and her chin on her hand, and looked at him. "Want to tell me about it?"

"No," he snarled. But Sarah just kept staring at him with those big blue eyes that were mirror images of his own and he sighed and gave in. "Yeah, maybe. Not that there's anything you can do about it." He pulled one of the ladderback chairs away from the table and swung it around, straddling it and folding his arms across the high back, his chin resting atop his arms. "I'm having woman problems."

Sarah's gaze widened in disbelief.

"You? That's impossible. Who is it?"

"She's new in town—you wouldn't know her. The problem is, I can't seem to get to know her, either. The woman doesn't hang out in any of the usual places. I can't think of a single, solitary way of getting to know her short of knocking on her door and demanding that she let me in."

"So why don't you do that? Knock on her door, I mean."

"Because I don't think she'd let me in. The only time I've seen her when she wasn't hurt or half-stoned from pain pills she definitely, but very politely, told me to get lost."

"Hurt?" Sarah stiffened and sat upright in her chair, staring at Trace with dawning realization. "This isn't Lily Townsend we're talking about, is it?"

"Yeah, how did you know?"

"Because I know you accidentally hit her with the Camaro and gave her flowers—and because she's a friend of mine."

Trace jackknifed upright in his chair.

"What?! You mean I've been driving myself crazy for a week trying to think of a way to see her again and all the time, you know her?" Trace was incredulous.

"Well yes, I guess so," Sarah admitted. "But I didn't know you wanted to see her. I mean, how would I have known—she isn't even blonde."

Trace snorted in frustrated disgust.

"What is it with you people, anyway? I haven't got some kind of fetish about blondes! I've dated women who weren't blonde."

"Sure," Sarah agreed with a complete lack of conviction. "Name one."

"Well, there was . . . !" Trace scowled at her, trying to remember, before he gave up with a shrug of annoyance. "I don't remember right now, but I'm sure I've dated someone who wasn't blonde."

Sarah rolled her eyes heavenward.

"Right—and I'm Princess Di in disguise!"

"Never mind the smart mouth; let's get back to Lily. Tell me all about her."

Sarah told him what little she knew, most of which Trace had already heard through the local gossip channels.

"I'm right back where I started," he growled in frustration, thrusting impatient fingers through his thick blond hair. "There's no way to see her without knocking on her door."

Sarah sighed and nodded.

"I'm afraid you're right. The only social event I've been able to talk her into attending is my wedding; she's going to be one of my bridesmaids. But that's not until Christmas."

Trace stared at her and slowly straightened, thick lashes narrowing with speculation.

"She's going to be in your wedding? So am I."

"I know—you're going to be Jesse's best man, but, Trace, that's nearly three months away."

"I know, but didn't you tell Jesse you needed to have that long because you had a million things to plan?"

"Well, yes, but . . ."

"And don't bridesmaids help the bride with all the preparations?"

"Well, yes, I suppose so, but I don't see how that helps you." Sarah looked perplexed.

"I'm a desperate man, Sarah. I'm even willing to use my favorite sister to see Lily."

"Hah," Sarah sniffed with derision. "I'm your *only* sister, so stop trying to con me and tell me what sneaky plot you're hatching in that brain of yours."

Trace grinned, blue eyes sparkling with anticipation and delight.

"Nothing, little sister, nothing. Not a thing. Of course, since you are my *favorite* and *only* sister, I'm willing to offer my services to drive you—and your bridesmaids—on errands, to appointments, to take you to lunch when your little feet are worn out from all the never-ending shopping you women do. In fact, I like you so much, little sister, that I'll even volunteer to take your bridesmaid with me and run your errands myself, just so you don't get so exhausted that you can't enjoy your own wedding."

Sarah stared at him for a long moment with an arrested expression on her face before she dissolved into laughter.

"Trace, you're incredible! Lily must have really bowled you over. You know very well that you *hate* to take me shopping!"

"Sure I do," he shrugged, broad shoulders moving inside the black sweatshirt with Iowa Hawkeyes emblazoned on the front, "but I'll do anything that gets me close enough to Lily to talk to her."

His words held a solemn, intense sincerity that surprised Sarah, and she eyed him for a long moment.

"Trace, I don't think Lily is like most of the women you date," she said slowly, trying to find a diplomatic way to express her concern for her friend. "I think she's been badly hurt in the past—she absolutely freezes up around men.''

''Has she said anything, told you why?''

''No, she's a very private person, and although we seemed to have an affinity right from the first, still, men and dating are not topics we discuss. Oh, she listens to me chatter on about Jesse until I'm sure I absolutely bore her to death, but she never reciprocates. It's almost like men simply don't exist in her life.''

Trace frowned thoughtfully, his gaze fastened unseeingly on the wooden tabletop.

''Well . . .'' he said slowly after a long, quiet moment had stretched into several minutes of silence interrupted only by the tick of the clock above the refrigerator. ''I suppose I should look on the bright side. If she doesn't talk about any man in particular, she's probably not involved with anyone. And if she's been hurt in the past and is avoiding men, then I'll just have to convince her that I'm an exception.''

''You sound . . . serious about her,'' Sarah said tentatively, blue gaze scanning the rugged features so like her own.

''Serious?'' Trace looked at her, and a slow smile curved his mouth. ''Oh, yeah,'' he drawled slowly. ''I think you could say I'm . . . serious.''

''Hey, Trace!'' Gavin's voice roared down the hall from the den. ''You just missed another touchdown!''

''Gotta go, sis.'' Trace stood and swung the chair back to the table. ''My team's winning!''

He sauntered out of the kitchen, whistling cheerfully.

Sarah stood and began to return to the refrigerator the food that he'd strewn across the tabletop and then forgotten.

''Hey, Sarah.''

She jumped and whirled around to see Trace standing in the doorway.

"You scared me to death," she said with asperity. "What do you want?"

"When are you and Lily running errands for this wedding?"

"We have an appointment for fittings the day after tomorrow—for our dresses—at Victoria's Garden."

"Great." He slapped the doorjamb and turned his back on her.

"Hey," she called after him. "How about putting the food away?"

There was no answer but the cheerful sound of a whistled rendition of "Proud Mary" fading away down the hall.

"Men!" Sarah muttered, and turned back to the refrigerator.

"Oh, Sarah," Lily's lavender eyes were mistily sentimental as she took in the ivory satin-and-lace gown, "you're going to make such a beautiful bride."

Sarah's eyes sparkled as she met Lily's gaze in the mirror. She glanced down and caught up the front of the satin skirt to reveal white Reeboks.

"Especially with these shoes!"

Lily laughed and shook her head, returning Melanie Winters' amused smile. The small fitting room was pleasantly crowded with the three women, and the full-skirted wedding dress brushed against Lily's knees where she sat on a small boudoir chair to watch the proceedings. The elegant owner of the shop was on her knees beside Sarah, a measuring tape draped around the neckline of her simple emerald wool dress, tailor's pins bristling from a little cushion on a band around her wrist.

"I sincerely hope you're not going to accessorize my

design with tennis shoes, Sarah,'' Melanie said dryly, her green eyes catching Sarah's gaze in the three-sided mirror.

''No, I promise I won't,'' Sarah answered, curling her toes in the comfortable shoes. ''But I must confess I'm tempted to wear them. I love the shoes I bought that match my wedding gown, but they have three-inch heels and by the end of the evening, my feet will be killing me.''

''That's okay,'' Lily teased. ''Jesse can carry you.''

''Hmm . . .'' A thoughtful expression moved across Sarah's features. ''That's not a bad idea.''

Lily and Melanie exchanged amused looks.

''Do you think you could make cummerbunds and ties for the groomsmen to match the bridesmaids' dresses, Melanie?'' Sarah asked, oblivious to the two women's indulgence with her absorption in her fiancé. ''I can't seem to find a tux shop that has just the right shades of red and green.''

''I'm sure I can,'' Melanie replied almost absentmindedly, meticulously measuring the drape of the left side of the voluminous skirt. ''How many will you need?''

''Hmm, let me see . . .'' Sarah began to tick off names on her fingers. ''There's Trace, Josh, Cole—if he can arrange to be free that weekend . . .''

She continued to name names, but Lily's attention was distracted by the sudden stiffening of Melanie's slim figure and the whitening of her fingers on the yellow tailor's tape when Sarah said her oldest brother Cole's name. Concerned, Lily glanced quickly at her face to find the usually calm, serene features pale, the emerald eyes dark with pain against the whiteness of her face. Frowning, Lily opened her mouth to ask if she was ill, but at that moment, the shop owner jerkily wove a last pin through the glossy satin and rested back on her heels.

''I'm sure that won't be a problem, Sarah. You can let

me know exactly how many you need when you've had some time to work up a final list. There,'' she said, giving the white satin skirt a final twitch and a last critical glance. ''That will do for today.'' She looked up at Lily. ''You're next, Lily. Your dress is hanging in the fitting room next door; I'll help Sarah slip out of this while you go change.''

''All right.'' Lily could almost have believed she'd imagined Melanie's reaction to Cole's name if it were not for the lingering paleness of her face and the faint tension still apparent in her slender frame. As she left the room, she made a mental note to ask Sarah if her brother and the green-eyed brunette had ever been involved.

The scoop-necked red velvet gown hanging on a brass hook on the dressing-room door had a long zipper up the back. It took Lily only seconds to peel off her emerald-green sweater and matching slacks. Standing in pink bikini briefs and matching bra, Lily unzipped the red dress, tugged it off the hanger, and stepped into it, pulling it up over her hips. She slid her arms into the close-fitting long sleeves and tugged at the zipper, but the slide caught in the net underskirt and wouldn't budge. She tried to move it back down, but it stubbornly refused to give way. Exasperated, Lily turned her back to the mirror in an attempt to see what it had snagged on. The thick mane of her hair swung loosely down her back and obstructed her view, and she swept it forward over one shoulder while she twisted, turned, and tugged, but the obstinate zipper wouldn't pull free. A soft rap on the door brought her head up with relief.

''Come in,'' she called, out of breath from stretching and twisting to struggle with the zipper. But the expectant smile on her face turned to startled surprise when, instead of Melanie's slim figure, Trace McFadden stepped into the dressing room.

* * *

"Your sister is in the back, Trace. Do you want me to let her know you're here?" The salesclerk smiled prettily at him, trying not to ogle the handsome, broad-shouldered man whom she'd sighed over a dozen times on the street.

"I think I'll just surprise her. Which room is she in?"

"Oh—well." Flustered, the young woman wasn't at all sure that she should let a male walk into the dressing rooms. "I'm not sure . . . That is, she might not be dressed . . ."

"Oh, that's all right," Trace smiled and said persuasively, "I'll knock first."

"Well . . . I suppose it will be all right. After all, she is your sister."

"True," Trace said dryly.

"Right through that door. The dressing rooms are on the left." The little redhead directed him to a swagged doorway in the back of the shop.

Trace ducked under the draped emerald silk and knocked on the first door on the left. A muffled voice bade him enter and he pushed open the louvered, white enamel door and stepped inside, only to draw up short with stunned surprise. Lily was standing facing him, her hair falling in a long sheaf of gleaming ebony over one shoulder and spilling almost to her waist. Her hair was black silk highlighted against a red velvet dress that was half falling off her shoulders, where pink satin bra straps crossed the smooth, faintly tanned skin. The mirror behind her reflected the long, graceful line of her back, and a narrow strip of soft skin was visible between the open edges of red velvet and the open zipper.

Stripped of her usual shell of cool composure by the unexpectedness of his arrival, astonishment kept Lily silent, her delicate brows arched above eyes dark and vulnerable with surprise. For one breathless moment, Trace thought he glimpsed a welcoming gladness in her eyes and the soft curve of her mouth, but then her features smoothed into cool lines, the lavender gaze going reserved and distant.

"Hi," he said quickly, before she could tell him to leave. "I'm looking for Sarah. Guess I got the wrong room."

Lily swallowed and drew a deep breath, unaware that the movement swelled her breasts against the red velvet and caused Trace to catch his own breath.

"She's next door."

"Oh . . ." He paused with his hand on the doorknob and lifted an inquisitive eyebrow at the way she clasped the edges of the dress together behind her back. "What's the matter—zipper stuck?"

"Yes, I'm afraid it is." Lily wished he would stop chatting and leave. She could feel the heat in her cheeks and knew she must be blushing. It was all she could do to keep her voice level and meet those blue eyes that watched her with an open male approval that she could feel all the way to her toes.

To her chagrin, her words brought him toward her instead of sending him on his way out the door.

"Turn around," he said with matter-of-fact calm. "I'll fix it."

"Oh, I don't think . . ." she protested, retreating a small step, but the small dressing room didn't allow room for maneuvering, and Trace merely caught her shoulders in his big hands and spun her around.

"No problem," he said, marveling that his voice still worked. The silky slide of ebony hair over satiny bare skin beneath his hand had his heart shuddering against his ribs. It was all he could do to keep his face poker smooth.

Facing the mirror, Lily fought down a sense of claustrophobic panic and stared at his reflection in the long glass as he bent his head, frowning slightly while he concentrated on the stuck zipper. His hands moved against the fabric of her dress, a fraction of an inch from the curve of her bottom. Lily would have objected, but his matter-of-fact attitude made a protest seem foolish. It clearly didn't bother him at all to be standing in this tiny room with her while she was half dressed. For a moment, Lily resented his casual attitude. No doubt it was a common enough occurrence for him, and she was probably only one of many women he'd seen with their dresses falling off their shoulders.

"Ah, I think I've got it," he said, and the backs of his fingers brushed warmly against her spine all the way to the neckline, just below her shoulderblades.

Lily stood motionless under his hands, but she couldn't control a shiver of awareness as his warm fingers moved slowly up her spine. Mesmerized, she watched him as his head lifted, those blue, blue eyes following the zipper's progress up her back until it reached the top. Then they lifted, his gaze meeting hers in the mirror.

The vulnerability underlaid with an unexplained fear in the darkened lavender gaze that met his sent Trace's hands stroking soothingly across the bare skin of her back to close gently over the outer curve of her shoulders.

"Lily," he said, his voice taut and thickened with emotion and worried concern.

Two sharp raps rattled the enameled louvers behind them and Melanie pushed open the door.

# THREE

"How are you coming along in here, Lily? I hope the dress—Oh!" Melanie broke off in midsentence, completely taken aback to find Trace in the tiny dressing room, his hands resting with familiar ease on Lily's shoulders. Green eyes widened in surprise and stunned shock and she turned a questioning gaze on Lily.

For once in her life, Lily's hard-won composure deserted her and she found herself at a loss for words. She, in turn, looked wordlessly up at Trace. Trace read the unconscious appeal in her eyes and his calloused fingers squeezed her shoulders gently, comfortingly.

"You must be the owner of this shop." Trace smiled at Melanie and held out his hand, his left palm still resting with easy possession on Lily's shoulder. "I'm Sarah's brother, Trace. I was looking for her and walked in on Lily by mistake."

Melanie accepted his hand silently, automatically, her face pale, her green gaze fastened on his face.

"Actually, it's a good thing he did." Lily had regained her composure, and with a slight, gracefully deft movement, removed herself from beneath the warm weight of Trace's hand and the fingers that moved in small, sensitive caresses against the silky curve of her shoulder. "I'm afraid I snagged the zipper on the net underskirt. If it weren't for Trace, I'd probably still be struggling with it." She threw a polite, vague smile in his direction and stepped forward to tug the door from Melanie's frozen grasp. "Thank you, Trace—you'll find Sarah next door, in dressing room number two."

Her meaning was obvious. Once again, she had very politely, very definitely, dismissed him. Only this time, he didn't plan to let her get away with it. He thrust his hands into his pockets and eyed her with wry amusement.

"Does that always work?" he asked with curiosity, lifting an eyebrow.

"Does what always work?" she replied with unruffled calm, refusing to acknowledge the challenge. Her gaze met his with only polite interest reflected in the lavender depths.

Before he could respond, the little dressing room was further crowded by Sarah, who peered over Melanie's shoulder and grinned at Trace.

"Hi, there, Brother, what are you doing here? As if I didn't know."

Trace ignored her knowing, teasing smile.

"Looking for you, actually. Jesse flew in earlier than he'd planned and he's at the house. I told him I'd track you down and send you home. He has something urgent to discuss with you."

"Really?" Sarah's teasing smile disappeared to be replaced with a concerned frown. "Did he say what it was?"

"Nope," Trace replied. "He just said he needed to talk to you as soon as possible."

"Oh, goodness, I hope it's nothing serious!" Sarah

spun on her heel to leave, but just as quickly turned back as she belatedly remembered Lily. "I'll come back and pick you up so you'll have a ride home, Lily."

"Don't be silly—I'll walk or get a taxi."

"I'll make sure she gets home, Sarah," Trace interjected smoothly, so smoothly that Sarah paused abruptly and shot him a quick, assessing glance. He returned it with an innocent, bland expression, and for the first time, she realized that in all likelihood, Trace had planned this. She wondered if Jesse really was at his house.

"Great, thanks, Trace, I really appreciate your offer." She decided to go along with what she was fairly sure was a complete charade, promising herself that if Jesse wasn't back in town, she was going to cheerfully wring her brother's neck. She slid the leather strap of her purse over her shoulder. "I feel just terrible about running off like this, Lily, but Trace will take you home."

"Don't worry about me, Sarah," Lily said, shooing her out the door. "I hope everything is all right."

"Thanks. 'Bye!"

And she was gone in a flurry of blue jeans and long blond hair. The silence that she left behind her held the trio suspended for a moment until Trace's deep midwestern drawl broke the tension.

"I'll wait outside for you, Lily, while you ladies finish whatever it is women do in these places."

"Thank you, Trace, it's kind of you to offer, but I really don't need a lift home," Lily said firmly, determinedly ignoring the charm of the crooked grin tilting the hard line of his mouth.

"It's no problem. I'm not working this afternoon anyway."

"Then I definitely don't need a ride—I don't want to spoil your holiday," Lily said softly, insistently.

*Stubborn little mule*, Trace thought, not without admiration. *She doesn't give an inch.* But he hadn't forgotten that torrid kiss in the hospital room and the revealing glimpse of the passionate woman beneath Lily's cool, protective shield. He wanted to see that woman again, and he was willing to do whatever it took to coax her out of hiding, so instead of arguing with her, he shrugged and stepped past her and into the hallway. The doorway was narrow, and Trace brushed against her as he went through it, hearing her quick, indrawn breath when his thighs grazed the red velvet. His gaze was fastened on hers and he saw the quick flare of response in the depths of her lavender eyes and the sudden bewilderment that followed before she dropped her gaze from his, hiding her response behind the thick fringe of black lashes.

*So, she's not as cool as she pretends to be,* he thought with satisfaction.

"Good day, ladies," he said softly, politely. "It was a pleasure meeting you, Melanie."

The shop owner fought back a surge of emotion. The broad-shouldered, blond-haired Trace was so like his older brother Cole that it was uncanny. The family resemblance was obvious in their facial features, but was even more pronounced in the depth of his voice, the way he walked in that sauntering stroll, and the easy smile that quirked the sensual male line of his mouth with its full lower lip.

"The pleasure was mine, Trace," Melanie managed to say politely, with a calmness that was a struggle to maintain. "I've heard Sarah mention your name so often, I feel as if I already know you."

"That's my baby sister." Trace grinned with unconcealed affection. "She thinks all of her big brothers are great. Just don't believe all the bad stories she tells you, only the good ones."

"Right." Melanie forced a light laugh.

"I'll be seeing you, Lily."

"Good-bye, Trace." Was it her imagination, or did his voice drop an octave and grow huskier when he spoke to her? Did those tawny lashes lower just a little while his eyes grew warmer? Or was it only that her own temperature rose several degrees whenever that blue gaze rested on her?

Both women watched as Trace strolled down the short hall and disappeared through the archway into the shop beyond.

Lily wasn't sure if she was relieved or disappointed that he didn't look back.

Trace leaned against the fender of the Camaro, arms folded negligently across his chest, legs crossed at the ankle, his gaze idly following the progress of Barbara Jean Turlow as she herded her four children into the five and dime, when he heard the bell attached to the door of Victoria's Garden jingle merrily.

His head snapped around to find Lily, clad in a soft emerald sweater and matching wool slacks, standing in the open doorway of the shop. Her hand clutched the knob of the lace-curtained door, sunlight glinting off her mane of satiny black hair and the small gold hoop earrings nearly hidden in the ebony thickness, while she stood perfectly still and stared at him.

*He didn't leave,* Lily thought, with an odd lift of her heart. The width of the sidewalk that lay between them gave her an opportunity to really look at him, all of him, that the small confines of the dressing room had not. She stared unblinkingly. He leaned with casual confidence against the gleaming orange fender of a classic '69 Camaro. The sleeves of a yellow cotton shirt were rolled up over strong forearms dusted with fine hair that gleamed gold against his teak-brown skin. The same gold sheen was echoed in the tawny mane that crowned his head. The blond strands caught and trapped the sunlight and fell over his brow above the dark lenses of aviator glasses that hid the turquoise glint of his eyes. Faded blue Levi's faithfully followed the line of strong thighs and long legs that ended with feet encased in scuffed, well-worn brown loafers.

Trace smiled, the lift of his lips creasing brackets beside his mouth, and when he slowly straightened and pushed away from the car, Lily snapped out of her trance.

"Hi," he said. His smile sent little shivers of reaction skittering up Lily's spine and ghosting over her skin, lifting the fine hairs that dusted the silky softness.

Wary of the response Trace was able to generate from her body, Lily retreated behind cool politeness.

"Hi," she answered.

"I waited for you," he said, hooking his thumbs in the back pockets of his jeans.

"I told you not to," she answered, not moving.

"I know." He grinned again, a cocky curve of his lips that alternately charmed and irritated her. "You'll find I don't often do what I'm told."

"Hmm." Lily lifted one eyebrow in imitation of his. "Does that always work?"

Trace laughed, a deep chuckle of appreciation.

"Do you remember everything I've said? And are you going to make all my words come back to haunt me?"

"No. And no—only if you deserve it." In spite of herself, Lily couldn't prevent the smile that curved the soft line of her mouth.

Trace groaned. "I think I'm in trouble! Let me buy you lunch and we'll negotiate a peace treaty."

"Thank you very much, but I'm afraid I can't."

Lily stepped out of the shop's doorway and pulled the door shut behind her, making the bells sound again with their cheerful jingle. She slid the strap of her purse over her shoulder and waggled her fingers in farewell before she turned her back on Trace and walked away down the sidewalk. Expecting an objection that didn't come, she counted seven steps before curiosity forced her to glance back over her shoulder.

Trace was walking behind her, his hands still thrust into the back pockets of his jeans while his lips pursed in a soundless, tuneless whistle.

Lily stopped and turned to face him, and he immediately halted some three steps away from her.

"What are you doing?" she demanded.

"Walking down Main Street," he answered blandly.

"Are you following me?"

"Yup, I sure am," he drawled unrepentantly.

"Why?"

"I promised Sarah that I'd make sure you got home." He spread his hands in a gesture of innocence. "I'm just keeping my promise."

Lily's gaze narrowed over the innocent expression on his handsome face, and she wished she could see his eyes behind those dark lenses. She was sure that if she could, she'd find laughter sparkling in the blue depths.

"This is ridiculous," she said, fixing him with a determined glare. "I told you—you don't need to escort me home!"

"Oh, but I do. I can't break a promise to Sarah. It would shatter her faith in me."

Lily was very sure that his concern for his little sister's faith in him had nothing to do with his persistence.

"Why is it that I have difficulty believing you, Mr. McFadden?" she asked him.

"I have no idea." He managed to look wounded. "I'm only concerned with your welfare."

"Right." Lily shook her head. "It's broad daylight, and I'm perfectly safe. So *go away!*"

She turned on her heel and walked away from him,

again, her hair swinging in rhythm to her determined steps, shifting silky strands to catch on the emerald-green wool of her sweater. Again, there was silence behind her, but when she chanced a glance over her shoulder, it was only to see Trace, some six paces behind her, sauntering along in the loose-limbed, easy stroll that did funny things to her breathing.

In exasperation, Lily glanced around, found that she was directly in front of the door to Kelly's Cafe, and ducked quickly inside.

A booth was vacant near the back of the small restaurant and she threaded her way through the tables toward the empty seating. With a sigh of relief, she slid onto the cool blue Naugahyde seat, but her escape was short-lived, for no sooner had she tucked her purse onto the seat beside her when the faint scent of aftershave reached her nostrils. She glanced up to see Trace dropping onto the bench opposite her.

"I'm glad you changed your mind about lunch," he said, and slid the sunglasses off the bridge of his nose and fixed her with an approving, warm gaze. "Frankly, I'm starved."

"I did *not* tell you that I would have lunch with you!" she said with frustrated exasperation.

"I know." He eyed her, trying to gauge the depth of her anger. Relief flooded him as he realized that she wasn't really furious. "But as long as we're here, we might as well eat, right?"

Lily tried to hold on to her anger, but even as she sought to drum up any real irritation, she felt it slipping away, hurried on by the hopeful, little-boy anticipation on his face.

"You really are impossible." She shook her head with exasperation. "Not to mention persistent. Don't you ever take no for an answer?"

"Not when it's something I really want." The blue eyes fixed her with a hot, intent stare that she couldn't look away from, the handsome face losing all of its teasing light as it went from laughter to solemn seriousness.

"What'll it be, folks?"

The waitress's gum-chewing drawl broke the spell that held them, and with an effort, Lily tore her gaze from Trace's and stared down at her menu.

"Have you eaten here before?" Trace's deep voice interrupted her dazed thoughts.

"No, no, I haven't," she said, looking up from the plastic-covered folder with its typed menu. "Have you?"

"Lots of times. Want me to order for you?"

Lily flipped the menu closed.

"Sure, why not."

Trace ignored his own unopened menu and looked up at the gum-snapping, teenage waitress.

"Two cheeseburgers with everything, cottage fries, and two double chocolate malts."

The young girl preened under his smile, taking longer than usual to scribble his order on her pad due to the many glances she shot him from beneath thickly mascaraed lashes.

"Will that be all?" she cooed at him, batting her lashes in a perfect imitation of a moonstruck calf.

"Yes, thank you."

The girl gave him a final, come-hither glance and left. Her seductive wiggle was wasted on Trace, for he didn't watch her, but Lily did. When he turned his attention back to Lily, she was staring past him over his left shoulder.

"What?" he asked, glancing behind him. But all he saw was the back of the retreating waitress and the small restaurant's half-full tables and booths.

Lily didn't answer immediately. Instead, she sipped her water, watching him over the rim of the glass with enigmatic violet eyes. It seemed impossible, but she would have sworn that he hadn't even noticed the young girl's attention. She shrugged mentally; it didn't really matter. When lunch was finished, she wouldn't see Trace again.

"What type of work do you do, Mr. McFadden?"

When she finally spoke, her question was so carefully polite and excruciatingly proper that Trace was silent for a long moment while he wondered what purpose was behind the tactic. Then he decided it didn't matter. All that really mattered was that, at last, she was actually talking to him.

"I restore classic cars."

"Really?" Despite herself, Lily was intrigued. She'd always loved old cars, especially the rakish coupes from the Elliot Ness–Al Capone era. "How interesting. Tell me about it."

"What do you want to know?"

"Everything. What's the very oldest car you've ever restored?"

"A Ford touring car from the twenties."

She scooted unconsciously forward in her seat, arms crossed on the tabletop, her face alive with interest while she listened. Trace couldn't doubt that her curiosity was genuine and he found himself telling her anecdotes about the many antique cars he'd worked on and their sometimes-eccentric owners.

The waitress interrupted him when she slid thick white crockery plates and tall soda glasses onto the tabletop between them. Both Trace and Lily sent her abstracted smiles and murmured thank-yous, and, disappointed, she left them to their food and conversation.

"Have you always restored cars for a living?" Lily asked curiously as she poured a pool of catsup on her plate and carefully salted her french fries.

"Mmmmh," Trace replied, his movements matching

hers as she absent-mindedly handed him the catsup and then the salt. "I worked for my dad in his auto body shop after I finished a hitch in the Army and college. I've always loved old cars, and when I told him I wanted to open a shop of my own, he helped me get started. I worked days for him and nights for myself until I got the business off the ground."

His voice held an unconscious pride in his work that carried clearly to Lily. She found herself wondering how he'd managed to build such a killer reputation with women when he must have been working twenty-four hours a day.

"It must keep you very busy," she said.

Trace looked up from his hamburger. She was sipping her malt, her lips pursed around the straw. He nearly groaned aloud. Speechless, he watched while she drew on the straw, her cheeks flexing as she sucked harder to draw the thick chocolate drink up through the red-and-white striped plastic tube. She glanced up and caught him staring fixedly at her mouth and she stopped swallowing.

"Is something wrong?" she asked him, uneasy under his stare.

"Uhhh," Trace paused to clear his throat, which somehow had forgotten how to form words. "No, nothing's wrong." *What could possibly be wrong? Just because everything you do reminds me of satin sheets and sex doesn't mean anything is wrong! At least, not with you. But probably, definitely, with me.*

He watched Lily lift her napkin and pat her mouth, but when he realized she was eyeing him warily, he forced his thoughts and his gaze away from the soft, lush curve of her bottom lip.

"Now it's your turn," he said, his voice deeper and faintly rough.

"My turn for what?"

"Your turn to tell me about your work," he replied,

the deep timbre of his voice smoothing out as he got his unruly body back under control. "Have you always taught school and directed Junior Symphonies?"

"No, not always, but there's really not much to tell you about my work," Lily shrugged with apparent indifference, but her fingers tightened on her napkin, twisting the paper into tortured wrinkles. "Besides, I doubt that it would interest you."

"There isn't anything about you that doesn't interest me."

Startled, Lily lifted eyes filled with quick dismay to meet the unfathomable deep blue of Trace's.

Trace understood the quick, wary analysis in the lavender gaze that met his, but he was taken aback at the very real fear that vied with dismay before she dropped her lashes and meticulously smoothed the napkin over her lap.

"Everyone in town is singing your praises for the work you're doing with the kids. Meg Stewart is ready to nominate you for sainthood any day now."

Lily glanced up to find the intensity on his handsome face had been replaced by a teasing, easy smile. Surely she was overreacting, and his interest in her was no more than he would feel for any other single, unattached female. Except for the bare-bones facts reported by the newspapers, he couldn't possibly know anything about her life after she left Los Angeles and before she came to CastleRock. She forced her muscles to relax and with deliberate casualness, picked up a french fry.

"Meg Stewart has a very talented daughter—all I did was give Kari encouragement and a few lessons."

"That's not the way Kari feels about you; she thinks you hung the moon." Trace saw the slight tremble in the slender fingers holding the catsup-dipped fry but pretended not to notice. Something was frightening this lady. Every time he ventured closer, she withdrew, allowing him a brief glimpse of vulnerability and fear before she quickly concealed any hint of emotion behind a calm stillness that would have defeated a less determined man.

"She's a sweet girl, and a very talented musician." Lily began to relax, unconsciously responding to Trace's retreat into nonthreatening, friendly interest.

"I understand you're also teaching music classes at West High," Trace commented, concentrating on his cheeseburger and only occasionally glancing at her. It was obvious that his attention made her nervous. He didn't mind that reaction, but it made him uncomfortable to think that her nervousness wasn't from awareness of him as a man, but from fear of something unknown to him.

"Yes," she answered.

"Do you like teaching?" Trace asked her curiously, reading her answer on her suddenly expressive features before she spoke.

"I love it." She waved a slender hand in the air, her face animated. When she talked about music, her face lost that remote, closed look. "Of course, I've always loved music, but working with these young people and introducing them to the magic of making music, helping them grow and stretch their horizons and capabilities—well, it's impossible to describe the pleasure it gives me."

"Do we really have that many talented kids in CastleRock?" Trace asked skeptically.

"Quite a few," she responded quickly, with firm conviction. "And even those who aren't as advanced as Kari are so eager to learn that it's a genuine pleasure to teach them. They soak up knowledge like sponges." She warmed to her subject, her lunch forgotten on her plate. "Children need music in their lives—and so do adults. Until the last fifty years or so, our society recognized that need, and most children were musically trained, both vocally and with an instrument. Musical societies were organized in every small town across America and communities gathered on a regular basis for musicals and summer Sunday afternoons in the park to hear the local band. Nintendo and television are poor substitutes for the social interaction and just plain fun people used to get from community choirs, symphonies, and Saturday-night gatherings at the parlor piano!''

Trace finished his lunch and watched with fascination while Lily's face lit with enthusiasm and he listened to her talk about her work. The rest of the luncheon crowd finished eating, paid their checks, and hurried out to return to their offices and shops, but Trace and Lily remained. It wasn't until the waitress had cleared the table and returned to refill their coffee mugs for the fourth time that Lily realized she'd spent nearly two hours in Trace's company.

''Oh my goodness!'' she gasped, glancing at the watch on her wrist. ''Look at the time! I didn't realize it was so late, I must have bored you to tears! Why didn't you stop me?''

Trace grinned at her with lazy appreciation of the sudden heat that colored her cheeks with flustered embarrassment.

''Why would I do that? This is the most fun I've had at lunch in ages. Usually I brownbag it with the guys that work for me or run across the street to Hardee's for fast food.''

Lily eyed him doubtfully. He lounged lazily against the blue Naugahyde-upholstered seat of the booth, exuding the same well-fed, relaxed, satisfied complacency that Lily had noticed in the gray-striped tomcat that adopted her the moment she moved into the little house she called home.

''Yes—well . . .'' She carefully replaced her coffee mug on the table and averted her gaze while she collected her purse. ''I enjoyed myself, too,'' she said, lavender gaze meeting his blue with clear honesty. "Thank you for the company. I really must be getting home now."

"I'll drive you." Trace set down his own cup and leaned forward.

"No." Lily reached out a quick, impulsive hand and touched his forearm, just as quickly retrieving it when she felt the warmth of his bare skin beneath her fingertips and palm. It had been a very long time since she'd touched a man; she'd nearly forgotten how vibrant and alive they felt. "Please, I really don't want you to take me home."

Trace tensed under her soft touch, his heart rate accelerating at the brief contact. He wanted to protest and refuse to let her go. But he decided he'd pushed hard enough for one day. Sharing lunch with him had been a major concession on her part and he knew it.

"Have dinner with me tonight," he said simply, unable to resist a final attempt, his gaze pinning hers. For once, that veil of secrecy didn't drop over her eyes, but he knew she would refuse even before she spoke.

"No, Trace. I don't date. It's nothing personal," she added hastily when she saw the growing frown and the rejection on his handsome face. A V drew down the arches of tawny brows. "I'm simply not interested in men, nor in relationships, nor in affairs. If I were, I'm sure you'd be first on my list. But I'm not."

"How about friends? Are you interested in friends?"

She shook her head, the black silk of her hair sliding forward over one shoulder. Slim fingers reached automatically to tuck the thick swath behind her ear.

"Not in men friends—only women."

"What have you got against men?" he asked. "A man can be just as good a friend as a woman."

"Maybe," she answered, refusing to give in to his cajoling, although to her surprise, she was tempted. When he looked at her with that intense blue stare, she could almost believe that he was sincere. "But I don't think so."

"Our situation is an exception to your rule," he said stubbornly. "I almost killed you. I feel responsible for you. How can I make sure you're okay if you won't see me?"

"I'm okay. You'll just have to take my word for it."

*But you're not okay,* Trace thought. *Someone hurt you, badly, and I'd give a month's pay to know the bastard's name. And for just five uninterrupted minutes alone with him.*

But there was a time to push and advance, and a time to retreat. Trace recognized by the stubborn set of her chin that this was one of those times when retreat was the best course.

"All right. I'll take your word for it."

Lily smiled in relief and slid out of the booth. Trace followed her to the small counter that held the cash register near the door. He wanted to insist that she allow him to buy her lunch, but guessed that she would refuse, so he stood quietly behind her while she handed the waitress her check and a ten-dollar bill. The crown of her head reached to just below his chin and he closed his eyes briefly, nostrils flaring as he inhaled the elusive scent of flowers that drifted upward when she shook her head at something the waitress said.

They parted outside the restaurant. Trace managed a casual good-bye and then stood motionless, watching Lily walk away from him down the sidewalk. He liked the way she moved, smoothly, with a light, graceful stride that set the long fall of black silk swinging gently against her back. His fingers itched to sink into the ebony mass, to test its softness against his lips.

His chest lifted in a deep sigh as he wondered how long it would be before he could think of another trumped-up excuse to see her. And see her he would, despite her refusal to consider even a friendly, platonic relationship. If anything, he was even more determined to get to know her better. Now that he'd had an opportunity to spend time with her, he was not only powerfully attracted to her physically, but the discovery that she was also bright, funny, and fiercely intense about her work exerted a powerful emotional pull.

All in all, he mused thoughtfully, Lily Townsend was a woman who appealed more to him the more he saw of her.

When she turned the corner at the end of the block and disappeared from sight, Trace sighed again, this time with regret, and whistling silently, turned to retrace his steps to his car.

It took Lily barely fifteen minutes to reach her little house. The 1940's bungalow sat amidst a patch of green lawn edged with a neat white picket fence. Lily had taken one look at it and knew she wanted to live there. After meeting little Miss Ida Mae Robinson, the landlord, she knew the house was meant for her and she paid the rent and moved in immediately. It was small, with only two bedrooms, but it suited her needs perfectly and she settled in with a feeling of cozy homecoming.

Lily pushed open the gate and walked up the flowerbed-lined front sidewalk, pausing to snap a wilted gold bloom from a shaggy chrysanthemum. The white wooden swing on the porch swayed gently as she passed, the chains creaking quietly in the afternoon heat. The screen-door hinges echoed the chain's quiet protest when she propped it open to unlock the front door.

The house enfolded her in cool silence, and Lily kicked off her shoes and padded barefoot across the hardwood floors to her bedroom. The old, brass-framed bed was covered in a candy-striped comforter in pink and white. A white lace tablecloth with a pink underskirt concealed a round, junk-shop table that served as a nightstand, and a huge green fern hung in a wicker basket above the table, its leafy fronds brushing against the sheer panels that filtered the autumn sun pouring through the windowpanes. The basic furniture had come with the house, but Lily had added her own things, together with junkstore treasures, to create a home stamped with her own personality.

She stripped off the emerald sweater and the matching tailored wool slacks and hung them neatly in the closet. It took only seconds to pull on jeans and a navy-blue sweatshirt, faded and comfortable. On her way out of the house, she stopped to pull open the refrigerator door for ice cubes and a pitcher of lemonade. She filled a glass and left the front door open wide when she went out, allowing the screen door to slap shut behind her as she walked across the front porch. Miss Robinson had approved her request to paint the porch planks and front steps a blue-gray to match the wooden shutters hanging neatly beside the tidy little windows. Lily dropped into the swing, one foot tucked beneath her, the other pushing restlessly against the blue-gray boards to set the suspended seat moving slowly back and forth. She sipped the frosty lemonade and narrowed her lashes against the intrusion of the bright afternoon sun.

The oak tree in the corner of the front yard had deposited another collection of red-gold leaves on her neatly trimmed grass, and when Lily drained the last of her lemonade, she decided to rake them into a pile.

Her efforts to stay busy and not think about Trace didn't work. Even as her arms reached and stretched and pulled on the rake, her rebellious thoughts kept returning to Sarah's brother. She mulled over the surprising and disconcerting attraction she felt for him. It had been a very long time since a man's presence had generated anything other than a wary defensiveness and revulsion. She took great pains to avoid interaction with men, especially men who were built like Trace McFadden—big, with work-hardened muscles that threatened her smaller, more fragile body. Despite the self-defense courses she'd pursued with grim purpose in the last five years, she still felt a mind-numbing fear of the sheer size and strength of big men. It wasn't an irrational fear; she had good cause to be afraid of a man's ability to overpower her smaller frame, and she feared the resulting pain and degradation that followed as surely as day followed night.

Thoughts of the lessons taught by Derek cast a pall over the sunny afternoon. Lily glanced skyward and was surprised to find the sun still shining in an almost cloudless blue sky. She shuddered and forced herself to clear her mind and concentrate on raking the leaves scattered across the lawn into neat, tidy piles.

# FOUR

Lily was on her hands and knees, her head stuck in the cabinet under the kitchen sink, when she heard the knock on the back door.

"Thank goodness," she muttered to herself, backing out from under the dripping pipes. She stood quickly and tossed a water-soaked towel into the sink. Water continued to leak in a steady stream onto the floor tiles from the bottom shelf of the cabinet, and her bare toes curled in objection to the cold puddle she stood in. "Yuk!" She grimaced and snatched up a terry towel to dry her hands while she hurried across the kitchen.

"I'm so glad you got here so quickly, the sink is—" She yanked open the back door only to halt in midsentence and stare speechlessly at the man standing on her back step, one brawny arm propped against the doorframe.

"Got a problem with your plumbing?" Trace asked, quirking an eyebrow at her. Laughter glinted in his blue eyes and curved the line of his mouth while he watched her try to find her voice.

"What are you doing here?" she managed to get out,

staring at his broad-shouldered, slim-hipped figure braced against her doorjamb with one powerful arm. He was dressed in black work boots, worn Levis, and a blue chambray work shirt with the sleeves ripped out. The edges of the torn seams were frayed, the faded, ragged edges trailing pale threads against teak-brown biceps. The shirt was unbuttoned halfway down his chest, the tails tucked into his jeans, and Lily's overloaded senses reeled at the view of sleek, sculpted muscles. A blue bandanna was twisted and rolled and tied around his forehead to serve as a sweatband and ruffled blond hair tumbled over it, brushing against his tawny eyebrows.

"Ida Mae called me. I always fix any problems she has with her rental." He pulled open the screen door and stepped inside and Lily moved backward as he advanced.

"But . . . but," Lily stuttered, waving the towel distractedly.

"What?" He stopped two feet inside the back door and eyed her. Hands propped on hips, he looked rumpled, earthy, disreputable, and faintly dangerous.

Lily swallowed. She badly needed the sink fixed. What little she knew about plumbing could be written in one word: nothing. She glanced across the room where the puddle from the dripping cabinet was slowly spreading toward them across the floor. She looked back at Trace. Even though he seemed no less pure male, the warm, affectionate look he gave her seemed to invite her to smile and share his delight that she needed him only three days after she'd told him emphatically that she wouldn't see him again.

She frowned, refusing to let him see that she was having trouble resisting his engaging grin.

"Nothing . . ." She gestured toward the sink and walked back to the cabinet. "I can't get it to stop dripping.

Actually, it's gone from a drip to a stream in the last hour."

"Hmm." Fortunately for her peace of mind, Trace didn't waste time crowing over his victory. He crossed the room behind her and bent down to peer into the yawning, dark cabinet with its leaking pipes. "Have you got some towels to mop up this water?"

"I'll get some." Relieved to turn the problem over to more capable hands, she hurried down the hall to the linen closet and came back with an armful of bath towels.

"Thanks," Trace mumbled distractedly before shaking them out and dropping them in a pile on top of the growing lake in front of the cabinet. He knelt, his head disappearing into the cabinet, and Lily watched him anxiously, holding her breath when she heard several clunks and a muttered swear word. He half withdrew and looked over his shoulder. "There's a box of tools in the bed of my pickup. Go get it, will you?"

"Sure," Lily replied, but he already had his head back under the sink and she doubted that he could hear her.

The late-model Ford pickup wasn't what she'd expected to find parked in her driveway. It didn't have the rounded, heavier lines of the thirties or forties model she would have thought Trace would drive. She stood on tiptoe to reach the toolbox and leaned to the left to balance the heavy weight while she lugged it up the back steps and into the kitchen.

Trace was stretched out on his back, his head and shoulders in the cabinet, knees bent. Wet patches darkened the faded blue of his Levis from knee to ankle. Lily looked at the pile of soaked towels that he lay on and thought guiltily that his backside was going to get just as wet.

The heavy toolbox clanked loudly when she set it down on the floor.

"Hand me a pipe wrench, will you?" Trace's voice

was muffled by the cabinet. One hand came out and waited, palm up, for her to comply.

"Uh, sure." Lily flipped the latch and lifted the metal lid. She stared in consternation at the collection of tools. "Trace—?"

"Yeah?"

"What does it look like?"

"Big. Has a red handle with black electrician's tape wrapped around the grip."

"Oh." Fortunately, only one big wrench in the box had a red handle and she removed it gingerly and placed it carefully on Trace's palm.

"Thanks," he mumbled, and the hand gripping the wrench quickly joined his other beneath the sink.

The hard muscles in his thighs flexed, the black work boots braced flat against the floor for leverage. While Lily watched, the whole line of his body strained, muscles rippling in his upper torso.

There was a clattering of metal against metal and a muffled curse of male exasperation from the depths of the cabinet.

"Are you all right?" Lily asked with concern.

"Yeah," he growled, aligning the slipped wrench on the stubborn pipe once again.

Again he braced and pulled, and the recalcitrant threads on the pipe gave in to a superior force.

He grunted in satisfaction and pulled himself out from the inside of the cabinet.

Lily backed up a step. Trace tossed the wrench into the toolbox and stood in one lithe, twisting motion, his back to her as he faced the sink. Her gaze ran quickly up his damp back, from his boots to the shaggy mane of tawny hair, returning helplessly to stare at the wet blue shirt and jeans that clung damply to the muscles of his shoulders, backside, and legs.

". . . so if this happens again, turn off the water right away."

"Hmm?" Lily realized that while she'd been staring at his body encased in clinging damp jeans and cotton, he'd been telling her something important and she hadn't heard a word.

Trace glanced over his shoulder. Lily was staring at him with a faintly unfocused look in her eyes.

*Hmm,* he thought he recognized the stunned expression, but decided to pretend he didn't notice.

"If this happens again, there's a water shut-off valve under the sink—" he repeated patiently.

"Will you show me where it is?" Lily interrupted.

"Sure." He knelt on one knee and beckoned her nearer. Lily sat on her heels next to him and peered at the U-shaped plumbing pipe, her gaze following his hand as it moved over the pipe to a round handle. "Here it is. Just turn it to the right until it won't turn anymore and you'll shut off the water. You won't be able to use the faucets until you fix the leak and turn the water back on, but at least you won't have your kitchen turning into a lake while you wait."

He smiled at her and Lily had trouble catching her breath. His blue eyes were warm, and much too close. Quickly she stood and took a step back.

"Yes, I see," she said breathlessly. "Thank you."

Trace levered himself erect much more slowly. He leaned his hips against the counter edge and crossed his arms across his chest.

"You're welcome." He just stood there, staring at her as if he planned to spend the afternoon absorbing her with that warm, appreciative look in his blue eyes.

Lily forced herself not to fidget.

"How did you get to be such an expert on plumbing?" she asked.

"Necessity." A smile creased laugh lines beside his mouth and eyes. "I own a house on Ithaca Avenue that was probably built around the same time as this one—and the plumbing is just as ancient. You get used to an old house's little eccentricities after you fix a few leaky pipes and creaking stairs."

"Well, I'm grateful that you knew what to do. I don't know a single, solitary thing about plumbing."

"Glad I could help, but if you're really grateful, you could fix me lunch. I skipped mine to come over here."

Lily started to shake her head in refusal.

"Please," he cajoled, ignoring the quick rejection he saw on her face. "I'm starving and I'll settle for anything—even a peanut butter sandwich. I have a one-thirty appointment with a distributor at the shop. If you won't take pity on me, I won't get to eat lunch today."

Lily glanced from his wet jeans to the repaired sink and back to his face with its expression of little-boy hopefulness. She couldn't turn him down; he'd done her a gigantic favor and if he'd missed his own lunch because of it, the least she could do was make him a sandwich.

"All right," she sighed and pointed at the little breakfast table with its two matching chairs in front of a window that looked out on the tidy backyard. "Have a seat over there and I'll see what I can find."

"Can I wash my hands first?"

He held up broad hands streaked with a mixture of grease, dirt, and miscellaneous rust from the pipes.

"Of course. There's soap in the blue dish behind you."

She turned away and opened the refrigerator door, rummaging in the interior and pulling out a variety of jars and a chunk of smoked ham.

Trace hid a grin of relief as he turned his back on her and scrubbed his hands. It took several soapings to get them clean before he rinsed and dried them, staring out the window over the kitchen sink at her backyard.

"You'll need to mulch those roses against the back fence before the first frost," he commented, running a practiced eye over the neatly trimmed bushes and raked leaves.

"Really?" Lily finished slicing two thick ham sandwiches into halves and took the plastic wrap from a bowl of potato salad before coming to stand a cautious twelve inches away from his elbow and look out the window. "I've never had rosebushes to take care of before. Where can I get mulch?"

"From my uncle Nate—he has a farm east of town. That's where my mom gets all her fertilizer and mulch, and she has the prettiest, healthiest rosebushes in town."

"I don't want to impose. Can't I just buy it at a nursery?"

"Nope, not as good as Nate's. Besides, he'd be insulted and get his feelings hurt if he knew you'd turned him down. He's real touchy about things like that."

Lily stared at Trace, trying to decipher if he was serious or if he was teasing her.

"How would he know?" she asked carefully.

"Well, I'd *have* to tell him," Trace looked scandalized, blue eyes dancing with amusement. "That's a slur on the McFadden family honor—having our mulch turned down. Not to mention our fertilizer!"

"I think *fertilizer* is the key word in this conversation," Lily said wryly, and turned away from him to pick up the plate and bowl and carry them to the table. "Come and eat your lunch, before I change my mind and throw it *and* you out my back door."

"Yes, ma'am." Laughter lay under the deep tones, but he followed her meekly and sat, tucking his long legs under the little maple table with its cheery yellow tablecloth. "Aren't you joining me?" he asked, looking at the single place setting.

"No, I already had lunch," she replied, avoiding his gaze while she transferred a bag of potato chips and a pitcher of milk to the table. She turned away and then abruptly turned back. "I didn't ask—do you want milk? There's iced tea if you'd rather have that?"

"No, milk's just fine," he assured her. She was acting as nervous and twitchy as a long-tailed cat in a roomful of rocking chairs. Trace ate his lunch and watched her bustle around the kitchen as she picked up the stack of wet towels, wrung them out in the sink, and disappeared with them into the small utility room off the kitchen. She reappeared with a mop and pail and Trace watched with unabashed appreciation as she swung the long-handled mop, stretching and twisting with sweeping, scrubbing motions. He'd seen other women wash floors, but it had never struck him as a particularly sexy exercise before.

Trace chug-a-lugged a glass of cold milk, wishing it were something stronger. The icy cold drink did nothing to lower his temperature.

Lily knew he was watching her. It made her nervous. He was always watching her. No one had to tell her that he was interested; even Lily, who avoided and ignored men's attention with a determination that bordered on paranoia, couldn't ignore Trace. To her irritation, she found that she was almost getting used to his attention and the butterflies in her stomach that accompanied it.

*He fixed my sink—I fed him lunch. We're even. Now I have to get him out of here.*

She returned the mop and pail to the utility room. When she reentered the kitchen, it was to find Trace draining his glass of the last of the milk, his plate empty.

"What time did you say you have to be back at your shop?" she asked, studiously avoiding his gaze while she snugged the rubber stopper into the sink and squirted dish detergent from a white plastic bottle into the stream of hot water.

"One-thirty." Trace gathered his dirty dishes and stood up. "But it's only a few minutes' drive from here. Why, are you trying to get rid of me?"

He halted behind her and reached over her left shoulder to slide his dishes into the water-filled sink.

Lily instantly stiffened. He wasn't touching her, but short inches separated his big body from hers, and the brief space threatened her sense of security. She drew a deep breath to steady her nerves and pulled in the clean scent of soap, the faint, sharp tang of machine oil, and a whisper of aftershave, all underlaid by an indefinable scent that spelled man.

Trace propped his hands against the tiled edge of the cabinet, bracketing her slim form between them. His face was only a few inches from the crown of her head and the silky braided rope of hair that swung against the yellow sweatshirt.

Lily spun to face him, fighting the surge of panic that closed off her throat and squeezed her chest.

Trace was too busy luxuriating in having her so close to recognize her fear. His gaze drifted over her face, noticing little details, like the little wisps of fine black hair that escaped from the braid to brush against her temples where a pulse beat beneath soft skin. Her ears, curved like the simple whorls of small shells, tucked neatly against her head, and tiny gold earrings pierced the small lobes. By the time his gaze brushed lower over the neckline of her sweatshirt and followed the slender column of her neck upward to find her mouth, Lily was shaking with tension.

His gaze shot from her trembling lower lip to lavender eyes filled with panic.

"Lily, what's the matter?" It didn't occur to him that

it was he himself that frightened her. He reached out a calloused hand to cup her cheek in an instinctive, consoling gesture.

"Don't—!" She knocked his hand aside. Beneath her fear, she was furious that she couldn't keep the tremble from her voice. "Don't touch me!"

Bewildered, Trace stared at her. He shifted his weight and would have stepped away from her, but she misread his movement and thought he was going to trap her against the counter. Instinctively, she moved to ward him off and her palms flattened against his chest.

Trace froze at the feel of her small, cold hands, still damp from the dishwater, against the bare muscles of his chest. His heart rate sped up, his breath catching in his throat. For a long moment, he couldn't register anything but the pure pleasure of having her hands on him, but eventually the fact that those same small hands were braced against him, her elbows locked in defense, got through to him.

"Hey," he said softly, this time reading correctly the fear in the wide violet eyes fastened on him. With slow, careful movements, he lifted his hands to shoulder height in a gesture of surrender. "I'm not going to hurt you—honest." He forced himself to take a step backward, regretting the necessity of the move that caused her soft hands to drop away from his body.

Lily dragged air into her starved lungs, trying to slow the slam of her heart against her ribs. Her hands fell to her side and she slid the palms down the denim covering her thighs in an unconscious effort to remove the feel of his warm skin. She swallowed jerkily, the brassy taste of fear strong in her mouth. How she hated it, and the memories that surged over her with the familiar taste. Trace was watching her with a new awareness in those worried blue eyes, and she groaned silently. She'd overreacted. The counselors had all told her that panicking at a man's closeness was perfectly normal for a period of time, but after five years, Lily thought she should be able to handle a situation like this with more aplomb. She could tell by the way Trace eyed her that he wasn't sure what to do next.

"I'm sorry," she said jerkily, smoothing a wisp of hair from her cheek with fingers that trembled.

"There's nothing to be sorry for," he answered, his deep voice softer, gentler. "I didn't mean to crowd you."

"It wasn't your fault," Lily said quickly.

"Sure it was." Trace shrugged his broad shoulders, his hands tucked into his back pockets. "I'm usually not so klutzy around women. I didn't mean to scare you."

"You didn't scare me," Lily denied immediately, her voice almost defensive.

"No? Good," he said readily. A smile quirked his lips. "Well, you sure as hell scared me! I tell you what, turn about's fair play. Why don't you pin me against the cabinet and make a pass at me?"

"What?" Startled, Lily stared at him. The lazy amusement in his eyes invited her to laugh with him, and held an apology for his earlier lack of sensitivity. Grateful for his calm acceptance and his willingness to laugh at what could have been a very uncomfortable, embarrassing situation, Lily smiled back at him. "I don't think so, not today."

"No? How about tomorrow?" he said hopefully, watching her with interest. "You could make me lunch again and have your way with me."

She laughed, a genuine throaty chuckle that clenched in his gut and warmed his worried heart.

"No, I don't think so."

"Well, anytime you're ready, just let me know." He pulled a beat-up antique silver pocket watch out of his jeans pocket. "Oops, gotta go, or I'm going to miss my appointment.'' He moved toward the door and pulled it open, pausing to look back at Lily. ''Thanks again for lunch. Call me if you have any more plumbing problems.''

''You're welcome—and I will, thanks.''

And with one last sexy grin, he was gone. Lily stared at the closed door for long moments before she roused herself and moved to take the remaining dishes from the kitchen table.

Lily was on her hands and knees, groping under her bed for the missing black ballet slipper that matched the one on her left foot, when a knock rattled the screen door onto the front porch.

''Drat!'' she muttered to herself, her fingertips finally catching the leather shoe. She pulled it out and stood, hopping on one foot while she slipped it on the other foot. ''I'm coming!'' she called, tugging down the hem of the blue angora sweater she wore over narrow-legged jeans.

She snapped on the lamp by the sofa as she passed through the darkened living room. The front door stood open, and through the wire mesh of the screen door, she could see a man's tall, broad-shouldered shape. For a moment, her heart stopped. But then she recognized the thick tawny hair gleaming under the porchlight and she breathed easier.

''Hi.'' She unlatched the screen door and pushed it open. ''What are you doing here?''

''Doing the neighborly thing.'' Trace leaned the point of one shoulder against the door frame and smiled down at her. Clad in worn, form-fitting jeans and a black sweater pulled over a white cotton shirt, he was big, broad, and somehow endearingly familiar. ''I came to borrow a cup of sugar.''

''A cup of sugar?'' Nonplussed, Lily stared at him.

"Yup, sugar." He waggled an empty cup, one broad finger slipped through the handle, at her.

Lily laughed. It was such a blatant, obvious fib that she couldn't help herself.

Trace managed to look injured.

"Don't laugh at me. This is a small town; all good neighbors borrow and lend—especially cups of sugar. It's your duty to lend me some."

"Heaven forbid that I fail to do my duty! What kind of sugar do you want?"

"Kisses," he answered promptly.

"What?" She eyed him as if he had just said *snakes*. "Is this another small-town custom? What are you talking about?"

"Kisses," he repeated with assurance. "Just like your grandmother used to get."

Lily just lifted a silent, skeptical brow at him.

"Don't tell me you didn't give your grandmother kisses!" he looked affronted and scandalized.

Lily ignored his melodramatics.

"I didn't have a grandmother," she answered with absolutely no expression.

"Oh." Trace decided to leave that flat statement alone for the moment, but filed her comment away with the many things that he planned to get answers for in the future. "Well, I had two. And both of them would come to visit and ask me for a little sugar. I was just a little tyke and I'd give them a big kiss—then they always gave me candy. Quite a bargain, I always thought. How about it, little girl, you give me a kiss, and I'll give you candy." He waggled his eyebrows at her suggestively and Lily had to struggle to keep a smile from curving her lips.

"I don't think so," she said. "Besides, I don't know if I believe that story. I doubt that you ever were a *little tyke!*"

"Oh, I was, cross my heart and hope to die." His finger crossed his chest in a big X and rose to pledge his truthfulness.

"Hmm," Lily eyed him skeptically. "You still haven't answered me. What are you doing here?"

"I came to visit." Trace hid his heartfelt hope that she would let him get away with this behind an earnest face. "Now, I know this may be a strange concept to you, but here in CastleRock, neighbors visit neighbors. I come to your door and knock, you answer it, you invite me to sit down and have some lemonade, and we sit on the porch and chat. Perfectly painless, see?"

Lily wondered if any contact with a man could be painless; but so far, Trace had proven to be completely different from any other man she'd ever known, and she was tempted to spend more time with him.

"All right," she said slowly. "You have a seat on the porch and I'll bring us something to drink. But I don't have lemonade. Is iced tea all right?"

"Iced tea is just fine." Trace smiled at her, his heart bounding with delight. He watched her walk across the living room and disappear into the kitchen before he slapped the door frame with a jubilant, satisfied palm and dropped into the porch swing.

Lily felt a moment of uncertainty. Was she being wise? Granted, Trace seemed trustworthy, and it was true that Sarah had complete faith in him, but was it safe to trust any male? All her counselors had told her that she needed to learn to trust again, and that not all men were like her ex-husband, but until now, she hadn't been tempted to put their theories to the test.

*What can happen on my porch, in full view of the neighbors?* she thought. *If I screamed, half the block would be in my front yard in ten seconds. Actually,* she reflected,

*Mrs. Carson is probably already watching from behind her curtains.*

Reassured, she finished pouring tea over the ice cubes in two tall glasses.

"Here we are." She pushed open the screen door with the toe of her shoe and let it slam gently behind her as she handed one of the glasses to Trace. "I put a teaspoon of sugar in it. Is that all right? I forgot to ask if you used sugar or took it black."

"That's perfect." Trace took the chilled glass and slid over, leaving room for her on the swing. "Now sit down."

Lily sat, curling one leg beneath her, leaving a good foot and a half of white painted wood between them. She sipped her tea and glanced sideways at Trace. He was drinking his own tea and seemed supremely comfortable and at ease. Somehow, his casual attitude when she was nervous irritated her.

"So," she demanded, almost militantly, "aren't you supposed to be *chatting?*"

Trace shot her a surprised glance, one eyebrow shooting upward as he assessed the stubborn set of her chin.

*Uh-oh,* he thought. *She's having second thoughts. Think fast, McFadden.*

"Yup, you're right, I am—supposed to be chatting, that is." He cast about for a safe, innocuous subject. Mr. Carson's sideyard, separated from Lily's lawn by the picket fence, held a tilled strip of ground, planted with vines and large, rounded lumps nearly invisible in the deepening dusk. Trace's glance lit on them with desperation, and inspiration struck. "What do you think of the pumpkin crop this year?"

"Whaaat?" If there was anything Lily expected, it hadn't been this.

"The pumpkin crop," he said blandly, with just a touch

of infinite patience in his deep tones. ''What do you think of the pumpkins? Mr. Carson's, specifically.''

''Uh.'' Lily knew that Mr. Carson was passionate about his pumpkin crop, but she'd thought he was merely eccentric. ''Nice, they're, uhmm, very nice pumpkins.''

Trace fixed her with a stern eye.

''Ms. Townsend,'' he said with emphasis. ''If you're going to be a part of this community, you're going to have to become acquainted with the finer points of our local history.'' He waggled his forefinger at her, and Lily crossed her eyes as she focused on it. ''Mr. Carson's pumpkins are coveted by every child in CastleRock. Not only does he grow the biggest and the best pumpkins in the county, but he also protects them with a twelve-gauge shotgun.''

''A shotgun?''

''Yeah, a shotgun. It's CastleRock's time-honored tradition that the kid who manages to steal the biggest pumpkin out of Mr. Carson's yard is the king of the hill on Halloween.''

''Really?''

''Really. 'Course, you have to share the crown with the kid who braved the CastleRock ghost to touch the hanging tree in the park. Unless, of course, you happen to have the honor of being the one and the same kid who did both.'' Trace eyed her smugly, clearly expecting her to ask him.

So she asked him.

''And were you the kid who had the *dubious* honor?''

''Yup. Actually I had to share with Jesse.''

Intrigued by this view of life in a small town that was so different, almost alien, from her own structured, ordered life as a child, Lily urged him on. ''So, tell me. How did you do it?''

Trace planted one foot in its scuffed brown loafer on the

gray floorboards and propped his other ankle across his knee, the fingers of one hand curled loosely around his ankle. He used the foot on the porch as a lever to start the swing moving slowly. And he told her. One story flowed into another as he told her of growing up in CastleRock, in the old Victorian house with his two brothers, sister, and parents, and of his long friendship with Jesse Lee James and the mischievous escapades of the two that had his parents tearing their hair out in frustration.

"Now it's your turn," he prompted a laughing Lily.

"My turn for what?" She wiped tears of laughter from her eyes and looked at him through wet, spiked lashes.

"Your turn to tell me about something outrageous you did when you were little."

Lily stared at him, consternation plain on her features.

"Goodness," she said slowly. "I don't remember ever doing anything outrageous. Mother and Daddy would never have allowed it."

Trace spared a brief moment to wonder just what kind of rigid people her parents must have been before he shook his head and smiled at her.

"Come on—you must have done something."

She shook her head. "Not that I can remember."

"No little kid is that perfect. Come on," he coaxed. "Didn't you ever snitch cookies out of the cookie jar? Write on the walls with crayons? Stay out after curfew and climb in the bedroom window?"

"No, the cook would have had a heart attack if I'd touched anything in the kitchen, and, besides, I don't think we had a cookie jar." Lily frowned, trying to remember where the French-speaking cook had stored the English biscuits that passed for cookies in the diet-conscious household. "And I was only allowed to play with crayons under supervision. I loved coloring pictures," she added wistfully, remembering the pleasure of splashing bright colors across the newsprint pages of books.

"What about climbing in windows?" Trace asked curiously, his sympathy aroused by the picture of a rigid household with no rule bending or allowances for a child's fancies.

"No, I've never climbed in a window in my life."

"Never stayed out too late on a date and missed curfew when you were a teenager, huh?" Trace smiled at her, that endearing, lopsided grin that did funny things to her heart.

"Never dated when I was a teenager," she answered absentmindedly, distracted by the creases his smile made beside his mouth.

Trace stared at her in astonishment, the hand holding his glass halting halfway to his mouth.

"*You* never dated when you were a teenager?"

"No." Lily realized he was staring at her in shock. "I was too busy. I didn't have time to date."

"Too busy doing what?"

"Working."

"Doing what?"

Was it possible that Trace really knew so little about her background? Lily stared at him for a long moment, considering whether she wanted to tell him, and if she did, just how much she wanted to tell him. Certainly not all; certainly not everything.

She decided to tell him a little. Just a little, just enough to satisfy the curiosity written on his handsome features.

"I was a concert pianist when I was a child, and when I was a teenager, I composed music."

"Really?" Trace watched her with fascination. "Sarah told me that you wrote music, but I didn't know that you did it when you were a child. What kind of music?"

"Pop, mostly."

"What songs? Would I have heard them?"

Lily smiled, a wry, self-teasing smile, before she named four song titles, three of which had made it into the Top Ten and one of which had been number one on the charts for a solid six weeks.

"Good God!" Trace looked at her with astonished respect. "I know every one of them by heart! They're classics!" Astonishment changed to baffled curiosity. "How did you wind up teaching school in Iowa? It seems like a long way from Hollywood."

"It *is* a long way from Hollywood," Lily answered noncommittally. She sipped the last of her tea and stared out across the dark lawn, past the picket fence to the street where city lamps glowed, dotting the residential avenue with alternating pools of gold light and dusky night.

Her voice held a sadness that tore at Trace's heart, but the finality that underlaid the husky tones silenced the questions he longed to ask. They sat without speaking, listening to the quiet night, until a police siren broke the silence with a far-off, halfhearted whirr of sound.

"Hmm, Mark must have caught a speeder out near the drive-in theater," Trace commented idly, cocking his head sideways to identify the location of the noise.

"I've never been to a drive-in theater, either," Lily said almost absentmindedly. "Another thing to add to the list of things I didn't do as a child."

"You've never been to a drive-in theater?" Trace's tones were disbelieving. "Oh, come on, they *must* have drive-ins in California!"

"I'm sure they do, but my parents never took me, and when I was a teenager, I was too busy—"

"You were too busy working. Yeah, I know." Trace shook his head at her. A look of determination shifted over his features and he bent, deposited his empty glass on the porch's floorboards, and with one lithe movement, stood and caught her hand to pull her up beside him.

Startled, Lily wobbled, the swing seat bumping against the backs of her thighs.

"Hey, what are you doing?"

"I'm taking you to the drive-in!"

# FIVE

"It's after nine o'clock," Lily protested, tugging on the hand enfolded in Trace's calloused palm.

"So? Movies at the drive-in don't start until after dark. Besides, it's a double feature, so even if we miss part of the first movie, we'll catch the second one."

"How do you know it's a double feature?" Lily asked suspiciously, reluctantly letting him pull her after him down the steps.

Trace paused to remove the empty iced-tea glass from her free hand and set it on the porch railing.

"Simple." He turned and dragged her after him down the sidewalk to the street. "They always have double features."

He pulled open the passenger door to the Camaro and gently pushed Lily inside. Even as she allowed his determined treatment, Lily wondered at her half-hearted objections. It had been years since she'd been alone in a car with a man, and part of her was amazed that she was seriously contemplating doing so now.

Trace rounded the hood of the car and slid beneath the

steering wheel. Immediately, Lily felt the dimensions of the car's interior shrink. Panic started to surge into her throat.

"I can't go to a movie, Trace . . ." she began. "I'm not dressed to go anywhere and I—"

"No problem," he interrupted her. "That's one of the great things about going to the drive-in; you don't have to get out of the car if you don't want to, so you can wear anything you like. Besides, you look terrific." He ran a quick admiring glance over the jeans and blue angora sweater she wore and grinned at her as he twisted the key and the engine turned over with a throaty roar.

Lily jumped, eyes widening.

"Fasten your seat belt."

She did so, fumbling the silver metal into the latch. The car moved smoothly away from the curb with a leashed power that had her fingers clutching the black leather edges of the bucket seat she sat in.

"This is like riding a tiger," she muttered to herself. The car purred throatily as if in response, and she glanced sideways at Trace. He was downshifting as they approached a stop sign, the muscles in his powerful thighs flexing beneath worn Levis as he depressed the clutch and brake pedal. Only the collar and turned-back cuffs of a white cotton shirt were visible under the black pullover sweater he wore, sleeves pushed to his elbows to leave powerful forearms bare. Thick, tawny hair was combed neatly, brushed back over his ears, the ends brushing against his collar at the nape of his neck. The warm confines of the car's interior were scented with the clean smell of soap and aftershave. Lily didn't feel entirely safe with Trace, but she was undecided whether it was Trace or her own ambivalent feelings that generated the feeling.

While she was questioning her motives, the Camaro moved them quickly across town and onto the highway.

Just past Big Eddie's Truck Stop, Trace turned into the drive-in.

"Oh, hey, this is great," he said with relish as he stopped at the ticket booth. He stretched, retrieving his wallet from his back pocket, and faded blue denim tautened over powerful thigh muscles. "It's a double set of slasher movies, and one of them is *Bloody Hands II*!"

Lily cast him a dubious, slightly revolted glance.

"Is that good?" she asked disbelievingly.

"That's great! Best kind of movies to see at the drive-in are horror flicks. Then you can scream all you want to, nobody cares."

"Oh, I see." Lily didn't see, but since he was the expert, she decided to withhold judgment.

Trace nosed the Camaro into an empty slot in the next to the last row of parked cars and fiddled with the speaker. A blast of sound responded and he turned it down.

"It works," he said with satisfaction, then he shoved open the door and jogged around to the passenger side to open Lily's door. "Come on." He reached in, caught her hand, and tugged her out beside him.

"Where are we going?" she protested.

"To the snack bar."

"But I'm not hungry."

"You will be. Besides, even if you're not, I am. I always eat my way through movies—it's tradition."

Lily groaned at the mention of another tradition. According to Trace, there were innumerable traditions in CastleRock. She doubted that she'd ever remember them all.

Fifteen minutes later, they were back in the car. A huge bucket of popcorn, dripping with butter and salt, sat on the console between them. An oversize red container of Coke and ice was turning Lily's fingers numb and she stared at the giant Butterfinger candy bar in her other hand.

"I have never in my life seen a candy bar this big," she said in amazement.

"No? Jeez, lady, you're definitely not a junk food person. I can see I'm going to have to instruct you on the finer points of junk-food addiction!"

She shot him a wry, amused look.

"Is this another one of those 'CastleRock traditions' you keep mentioning?"

"Nope." Trace fiddled with the volume knob on the speaker. "Just mine. But don't ever let my mother know. She goes into cardiac arrest if anyone mentions junk food. She's a health food freak."

"I know," Lily responded. "Sarah told me."

"Uhmm." Trace finished adjusting the speaker's sound level and settled back in his seat. He tossed a handful of popcorn into his mouth. "Hand me a napkin, will you?"

Lily passed him a napkin and wriggled into a more comfortable position. For long moments, silence reigned in the car, punctuated only by the movie's soundtrack. On the screen, an incredibly ugly, monstrous sea creature was creeping up on the unsuspecting hero. It reached him and wrapped grotesque arms around his body.

"Yuk!" Lily burst out, grimacing as blood spurted and flesh gave way in graphic, gory detail. "This is disgusting!"

"Yeah," Trace answered. "Isn't it great!"

"Great?" Lily turned to stare at him. He was facing the screen, avidly watching the monster dismember the hero. "You're watching a man being ripped limb from limb and you think it's great? You're a very sick person, Trace McFadden!"

"Hey . . ." Trace complained, eyeing her slim figure. "This is the part where you're supposed to be so terrified that you throw yourself into my arms so I can protect you from the big bad monster."

Lily was suddenly, vividly, painfully aware of how small the interior of the car was and how close Trace's big body was to her own. She knew he wanted to kiss her; she could see it in those blue eyes that had gone lambent as they drifted over her face and fastened intently on her mouth. Her lips went dry and she ran her tongue over them to dampen them. Flames flickered in the depths of Trace's eyes and panic gripped her. She hurried into speech.

"I'm not sure I'll ever get used to all the traditions of CastleRock. Maybe you need to be born here to learn them all."

Her words were rushed, almost tripping over each other as she spoke, and the normally low musical voice held a faint tremble. Trace noticed, and privately cursed whoever had hurt her and made her fear men and the slightest of intimacies. With elaborately slow movements, he picked up a handful of popcorn and tossed it into his mouth as he faced forward again to watch the screen.

"Nah, I don't think so. You'll learn. We'll just have to break you of all those big-city habits first."

Relieved at the change of subject and the suddenly defused situation, Lily sipped her Coke, the cold liquid running down her parched throat.

"What big-city habits?"

"Turning up that cute nose at really great monsters, for one thing—and look at this!" He pointed at the screen, drawing Lily's attention back to the slimy creature and eliciting another groan of disgust. He laughed, his eyes crinkling at the corners at the look of revulsion on her face.

"You're impossible," she said with mild heat, shielding her eyes behind her fingers, peeking out as a particularly loud shriek issued from the speaker.

"Yeah, but I'm fun," he grinned at her unrepentantly.

She sniffed and peeked at the screen again, amazed at the many varied ways the movie's director had conceived to separate human body parts. *He's right,* she thought to herself. *He is fun. And I haven't had fun in a long, long time.* Surely it couldn't hurt. Trace McFadden was a man who enjoyed women. He wasn't interested in long-term commitments, any more than Lily herself was. Surely it couldn't do any harm for her to enjoy his company; he'd already proved that he wouldn't push her if she didn't want him to touch her. Lily decided to relax and enjoy herself.

It was nearly midnight before Trace pulled the Camaro into the curb in front of Lily's little house and walked her to her door. He held the door open for her and Lily stepped inside, pausing to turn and face him.

"Thank you, Trace, I had fun tonight."

"Hey, no problem, it was my pleasure." He looked down at her upturned face, pale in the glow of the amber porchlight, and felt an unfamiliar emotion grip him. He wanted to touch her so badly that he ached. He wanted to bend down and take her mouth beneath his, to know her taste and the feel of her lips beneath his. He'd wanted other women, but never with this mixture of lust and an emotion that made his hands tremble with want and need. "Lily," he said, his voice rusty, rasping over a throat constricted with emotion. "I know you're not ready to hear this, but I want to kiss you good night. I also know that you don't want me to and that you're afraid to be touched," he went on, ignoring the worried alarm that moved swiftly across her features. "And I want you to know that I won't push, but anytime you're ready, all you have to do is say so. Anytime you want to kiss me, feel free. Or touch me. Anywhere, anytime, anyplace."

Lily stared at him, overwhelmed by his restraint and gut-wrenching honesty. Intense blue eyes held hers with an unmasked emotion that shook her and demanded an answering, equal honesty.

"Trace . . ." she began helplessly, her voice faltering before she could steady it. "I don't want to deceive you. I don't think I'll ever be able to voluntarily touch a man, or let him touch me. I can't even imagine wanting to kiss a man."

Trace reeled under her declaration, even though it confirmed what he already suspected. A dozen questions raced through his thoughts, and uppermost was the need to demand the name of the son of a bitch who had hurt her. But he suspected that this was the first time Lily had confided as much to any man and he didn't want to break that fragile bond of trust, so he fought down his own instinctive urge to punish anyone who had hurt her and, instead, focused on her.

"All right," he said, his voice deeper, husky with emotion, "then I'll wait till you're ready, and I'll try to change your mind."

"I don't think I'll ever be ready." Lily felt like crying.

"Hey . . ." His voice softened, gentled, as tears misted the wide violet eyes fastened intently on his. "I didn't mean to make you cry." He forced a smile and winked at her. "Wait and see, you're going to like kissing me as much as you *loved* that blood-and-guts movie tonight."

"Ick," she said, managing a shaky smile of her own. "That's not a promise, that's a threat."

"No," he said slowly, his gaze flicking to her soft, trembling mouth and back up to her eyes. "That's definitely a promise."

She stared at him, unable to think of a response, half afraid of the promise of pleasure implicit in his softly spoken words and the heat in his blue eyes, half trembling with the anticipation of his promise.

"You better get some sleep if you're going to face those

kids tomorrow,'' he said gently, not unaware of the mixed emotions clearly visible on her expressive face. ''Lock the door.''

''Good night,'' she said softly.

''Good night.''

Lily closed the door slowly, the latch clicking quietly.

''Lock it.'' His deep voice carried easily through the wood and glass.

Lily slid the deadbolt home.

''Good night, honey.''

''Good night, Trace,'' she said just as softly, and listened to the soft thump of his steps as he crossed the wooden porch. She inched back the sheer curtain gathered on its rod over the oval window in the top half of the door. The streetlight pooled around the Camaro and glinted off Trace's hair as he crossed the sidewalk and skirted the car's hood. The car door closed with a solid, audible thunk and, seconds later, the powerful engine turned over with a muted growl before the car slid away from the curb and disappeared down the street. Lily watched the red brake lights flicker at the corner and the car disappear from view before she let the curtain drop and walked slowly through the quiet, darkened house to her bedroom.

That was the first of many evenings that saw Trace appear unannounced on her doorstep to charm his way inside or cajole her into going out with him. The week before Halloween found the two, accompanied by Sarah and Jesse, bundled up against a brisk afternoon wind, picking out pumpkins at Trace's uncle's farm east of CastleRock to carve into jack-o'-lanterns.

Nathan McFadden was a spry, eighty-three-year-old. Dressed in striped Oshkosh overalls over a blue wool shirt, a flannel-lined denim Levi jacket, brown Wellingtons on his feet, and a billed cap covering his white hair, his high

Norwegian cheekbones and piercing blue eyes were older versions of his nephew Gavin's. He came out of the two-story white farmhouse to meet them, a shaggy collie trotting at his side.

" 'Bout time you young'uns showed up," he commented in response to their greetings as they piled out of the Camaro. "Your mom's been pesterin' me for days about savin' the best pumpkins for her."

"She gave us strict orders about the size and shape she wants." Sarah stood on tiptoe to kiss his weathered cheek and Lily saw the gleam of affection deep in his blue eyes even as he cleared his throat gruffly.

"Well, come on, come on," he growled, and snapped his fingers at the collie to come to heel. The dog quickly deserted Lily's stroking hand over her silky head and trotted to the old man's side. "Decided to plant 'em on the east side of the barn this year for a change. They seem to have done right well there."

The four trooped after Nathan's erect figure, across the barnyard to a gate in the fence that stretched from the corner of the big red barn down the lane to the highway. Nathan opened the gate and held it until they were all through before latching it behind them.

"You pick out however many you want," he instructed, "and be sure to get some for your mom."

"Aren't you going to help us, Nathan?" Trace asked, pausing when he realized his great-uncle was on the wrong side of the fence.

"Nope, got no time for that today. You're on your own," he responded with a brisk shake of his head. "I got me a ballgame to watch on television."

"Hey, that's right, the Hawkeyes are playing today!" Jesse and Trace's faces lit with identical expressions.

Sarah shot a long-suffering glance at Lily and caught Jesse's arm in both hands to tug him into the field.

"We're picking out pumpkins, remember? Not watching football."

"Yeah, you're right." Jesse grinned down at her and let her pull him down a row of reddish-orange pumpkins between the remnants of harvested dried corn stalks.

"I like Nathan," Lily commented, bending to inspect a potential jack-o'-lantern. It turned out to be misshapen on one side and she deserted it to move farther down the row.

"You just like his fertilizer," Trace teased, watching with appreciation as she bent over to look at a pumpkin and her jeans snugged tighter over her bottom.

"True," she laughed and looked over her shoulder at him, but by then Trace was industriously poking at the vines and shifting their orange globes. "You were right. Even the man at the nursery told me that the mulch we got from your uncle Nathan's farm was the best thing for my rosebushes."

"See? I told you so," he said with satisfaction.

Lily watched Trace kneel on one knee and roll a fat orange pumpkin on its side to check the bottom for color.

"I thought you told me that stealing pumpkins from Mr. Carson was the only way to get a Halloween pumpkin?"

"It was. But I had to give it up after I got older. The twelve-year-olds didn't like the competition." Trace looked up at her and grinned. An answering grin curved her mouth and sparkled in the depths of violet eyes. A vagrant breeze teased strands of silky black hair, tossing them across her face to cling against glossed lips. Her slim, gloved fingers absently pushed the ebony strands back over her shoulder. Earmuffs of soft white rabbit fur protected her ears from the wind, and a matching white scarf was wound around her throat over the collar of her scarlet wool jacket. Her cheeks were rosy with the cold and wind and she looked vibrantly healthy and happy.

Gone was the reserved, haunted woman Trace had seen in the hospital room, and he knew a deep burst of pleasure that he had helped banish, at least for the moment, that other Lily.

"Hmm, you don't look much older than twelve right now," she observed, unaware of his thoughts while she eyed his wind-tossed blond hair and wind-reddened cheeks. She was freezing, but Trace didn't seem to feel the cold. His beat-up high school letter jacket in blue wool with its cream leather sleeves was unsnapped and hung open down his chest and beneath it he wore only a blue plaid flannel shirt with a gray sweatshirt pulled over it. The usual worn Levi's clung to the hard lines of his thighs and calves and beat-up sneakers covered his feet.

"Oh, yeah?" He lunged to his feet and growled and she ran, shrieking with laughter, across the stubbled corn field, leaping over pumpkins and vines with him following close on her heels, until she dodged behind Sarah's bundled-up figure.

Later that night, snuggled beneath the thick comforter on her bed, Lily smiled sleepily, remembering the childish silliness they'd indulged in. *Trace was right.* She smothered a huge yawn. *He really is a lot of fun.* As she drifted off to sleep, she was barely aware of the melody that moved through her subconscious, teasing her, coaxing her to remember the familiar fountain of music that had charmed her childhood and always shared her dreams. But Lily's conscious self, bereft for so long at the disappearance of the music that had woven its way since birth into the fabric of her life, wasn't yet ready to acknowledge the return of the magic. So she slept peacefully, and dreamed of Trace and the warm security she felt with him and in her dreams, the music played, unrestrained and growing quietly, gloriously stronger.

* * *

"I can't make it to dinner tonight, Lily." Trace's voice was regretful.

"Why not?" Lily tightened the phone receiver over her ear and put a palm over her other ear to block out the noise from the students changing classes in the hallway outside West High's administrative offices. Her own voice held disappointment.

"I have to work . . ." His sigh came clearly over the phone line. "I probably won't be finished before midnight."

"Are you going to work through dinner?" she asked.

"Yeah, I'll probably grab a hamburger later; I usually get starved around nine o'clock."

"You shouldn't work all day and then only eat junk food," she chided softly.

"I know," he chuckled, the deep sound rippling up her spine. "Don't tell my mother, she'll have a fit."

"All right, but in good conscience, I'll have to give you a lecture about vitamins and nutrients and . . ."

Trace groaned, the smile that curved his mouth invading his voice.

"Do you have to? I've heard this a thousand times!"

"Clearly, you haven't been listening!"

"True," he admitted, grinning and foolishly happy at the teasing laughter in her husky voice.

"Hey, Trace," Charlie called behind him. "The delivery truck's here with the transmission for the '49 Chevy!"

"I gotta go, honey." He didn't want to, he could willingly and happily lean against the wall of his small, cluttered office all afternoon and listen to her voice. He damned to perdition the balky transmission that refused to cooperate and the equally balky owner that demanded the Chevy a week before the original delivery date.

" 'Bye, Trace," Lily said softly.

" 'Bye, Lily," he said just as softly, and reluctantly

hung up the phone. He stood motionless and stared at the silent black instrument for several long moments until Charlie's call once again demanded his attention. "Yeah, I'm coming," he yelled back and left the office.

For the tenth time in the last ten minutes—the same ten minutes it had taken her to drive across town from her house to Spring Street and park outside the building housing McFadden Classic Cars—Lily had second thoughts. And third thoughts, and fourth and fifth, about the wisdom of her spur-of-the-moment decision to bring Trace dinner. Fraught with indecision, she sat in her car across the street from Trace's shop and stared at his building.

The garage took up at least a fourth of a block, and although it was an older building, it was well maintained and tidy with new paint. The sign over the wide doors that spelled out McFadden Classic Cars was lettered in simple classic black against white. Lily wondered fleetingly if Jeannie's artistic hand had planned the sign and thought it distinctly possible. The sign on the office door read "closed," but a light glowed through the small, square windows set high in the big garage doors.

*Don't be such a chicken,* she chided herself. *Bringing a man pizza when you know he skipped dinner is a friendly, neighborly thing to do.* Still, it didn't matter what reason she used, she knew very well that she was sitting outside Trace's garage because she missed him. Bringing him dinner was just an excuse.

With sudden decision, she picked up the pizza box and the liter of Pepsi from the seat beside her and got out of the car. Her breath puffed out in frosty little clouds into the cold air as she hurried across the street, and she wondered briefly if the overcast, dark night sky would deliver on its threat of snow.

The office door was unlocked when she tried the knob. The sound of a radio blaring from within the depths of the garage reached her ears and she passed through the dimly lit office and the door on the far side to step into the work area. The high ceiling gave the huge room a cavernous feeling, and three antique cars, in various states of repair, filled the floor space. A waist-high bench ran around the wall on three sides, and tools hung above it on the walls. The radio sat on a shelf near a window on the far side of the room, and Lily realized that beneath the distinctive lead guitar of Mark Knopfler and Dire Strait's "Money For Nothing" was the sound of metal against metal.

"Damn it!"

She smiled as she recognized Trace's deep, irritated voice and walked around two of the cars. The third car was an old Chevy, and Lily instantly recognized the black lace-up boots and long legs protruding from under the frame. She sat on her heels and peered under the polished burgundy chassis.

"Hello there."

"Ouch!" Startled, Trace reared up and smacked his forehead against the frame. "Damn it!" He rubbed his aching head and squinted to look past his long legs and found Lily's laughing face.

"Hey!" He grabbed the frame and slid out from under the car, looking up at her with astonished delight. "What are you doing here? Not that I'm complaining, mind you," he added hastily.

"I brought you junk food," she said, easily reading his face and finding only unreserved pleasure to see her. "But it's pizza. Which as you know," she added sternly, eyes twinkling, "is the only junk food I know of which even your mother has to admit has *some* nutritionally redeeming value."

"Bless your heart," Trace said fervently, inhaling the

mouth-watering smell of melted cheese and pepperoni with a look of near bliss. "I'm starving!"

"Good!" Lily stood and watched him roll to his feet with agile ease. "Where shall I put this?"

"Over there on the bench. I'll wash up and be right with you."

He loped off across the garage and Lily turned to clear a place on the tool-cluttered workbench. Gingerly, she lifted a greasy piece of black metal and moved it to one side, shifting several wrenches and screwdrivers to the opposite direction to make a space for the pizza in its cardboard box.

"Do you have any glasses, Trace?" she called.

He stuck his head out the open door of the bathroom. "No, but there are some extra coffee mugs in here. You want them?"

"Yes," she answered, and circled the cars. She stood in the doorway of the restroom and peered in. "Yuk!" She wrinkled her nose at the black oil-and-grease-spattered sink. "You need a cleaning lady."

"We don't get many ladies in here, cleaning or otherwise," he said, blue eyes lighting with amusement at the offended look on her delicate face. He fought down an urge to lean down and drop a kiss on the tip of her nose. He was so damn glad she was here, he could hardly control his elation. Especially since she had sought him out, without his insistence and cajoling. He felt like a kid on his first trip to an amusement park, high on happiness.

"Hmm," she commented, and leaned past him to take two clean mugs from the half dozen sitting upside down on a paper towel on a shelf just below the small mirror. She glanced down at the black water running off his hands and into the sink and opened her mouth to ask him if he thought he could actually get all the grease off his fingers, when she glanced past him and saw the poster tacked on the wall.

Trace saw her gaze move past his shoulder and her eyes widen in reaction and knew instantly what she was looking at.

"That's not mine," he denied, and shifted so that his broad shoulders nearly blocked her view of the full-color blow-up of an almost nude, incredibly busty blonde. "It's Charlie's."

Lily looked at him without comment for a moment. Then, to his relief, mischief sparkled in her lavender eyes.

"Really?" she asked with innocent inquiry. "But she's blonde. Are you sure that's not your poster?"

Trace groaned and eyed her threateningly.

"Not you, too! Have you been talking to my sister?"

"About what? Trace McFadden's blondes?" she asked, batting her eyelashes at him with exaggerated movements. "Don't you know that's a *tradition* in CastleRock?"

Trace bit off an uncomplimentary word that told her bluntly what he thought of this particular *tradition*.

"Get out of here and let me wash my hands in peace, or I won't let you have any of my pizza," he threatened, and grinned as she sauntered blithely away, cups in hand. For a brief moment, he watched the feminine confidence in her saucy stride and wondered if maybe, just maybe, she was ready to deepen their relationship. Because whether she was willing to admit it or not, they *did* have a relationship; her coming here tonight underscored that fact, and subtly hinted that she was moving closer to admitting it.

*Don't push,* he told himself, reluctant to make a move that might send her running to hide behind the cool wall she was so adept at setting up. For the first time, his pleasure at seeing a woman happy overrode the physical need for her that alternately tormented and teased him.

Lily watched Trace exit the restroom and walk toward her, drying his hands on paper towels that he paused to toss in a battered garbage can as he approached. A streak of black grease marred his forehead below tawny hair, and oil stained his blue chambray shirt and jeans. He was the complete antithesis of other men she'd known. His big, brawny body was the result of hard work, not workouts in trendy gyms, and his hands were calloused from use instead of being soft and white as her own. There was an elemental maleness in him, coupled with a gentleness that made her feel safe and urged her to curl close to his welcoming warmth. The pleasure that lit his blue eyes every time he looked at her made her feel wanted and treasured, feelings so alien that she was continually surprised by them.

"Where's my pizza, woman?" he demanded in a threatening growl that was completely spoiled by the grin that tilted his mouth.

"Right here." Lily handed him a wide slice on a napkin and laughed as he took a bite, and his eyes rolled upward in an expression of bliss.

"This is great," he said past a mouthful of cheese, crust, and pepperoni.

Perched on a high wooden stool, Lily watched him quickly demolish two-thirds of the large pizza and wash it down with half of the liter bottle of Pepsi.

"You weren't kidding," she commented, smiling as he wiped his mouth on a napkin and stretched with the lazy, contented movements of a well-fed cat.

"About what?" he asked, turning to toss the crunched napkin at the trash can.

"About being starved."

"Heck, no." He patted his flat stomach. "I haven't eaten since noon and I'm a growing boy."

"A growing boy?" Lily lifted one fine-arched brow,

lilac eyes skeptical. "Just how much more are you planning to grow?"

"When I was a kid, I decided I wanted to be as tall as the Jolly Green Giant. Remember those commercials?"

"Yes, I remember. But why did you want to be as tall?"

"To tell you the truth, I think I really wanted to be green," Trace grinned at the laughter that convulsed Lily. "Hey, what can I say? I think I was about five years old at the time. Being green was really cool."

"Your poor parents—have you told them that your big goal in life is to be thirty feet tall and green?"

"Nah, they probably think I outgrew it; let them think I'm halfway normal." Trace loved the way her eyes crinkled when she laughed and her face lit with amusement. "Come on, confess, what did you want to be when you were five years old?"

"Hmm, let me see . . ." She narrowed her eyes consideringly. "If I remember right, I was already practicing piano four hours daily and I wanted to be Peter Pan and fly off to Never-Never Land where children played all day and never had to grow up."

"Oh, yeah? How come you didn't want to be Wendy?" he asked, as always, the reality of how little childhood she'd enjoyed hitting him with blunt force.

Lily wrinkled her nose disparagingly.

"She had to play little mother and watch out for the younger ones. I wanted to be Peter Pan and have adventures, like dueling with Captain Hook."

"Great book, wasn't it? Did you read a lot when you were little?"

"Yes, I loved books. Did you?"

"Sure, everybody in the family reads a lot. My favorites were Rafael Sabatini's *Captain Blood* and Jack London's *White Fang*."

"Oh, I loved those, too!" Lily leaned forward on her stool, her features vivid with discovery. "Did you read the Walter Farley Black Stallion books and Albert Payson Terhune's dog books?"

"Most of them, but before I finished all the library had stocked on their shelves, somebody loaned me a copy of Ursula LeGuin's *Earthsea Trilogy* and I got hooked on sci-fi fantasy for a while."

Entranced, Lily listened while he talked about the books he'd read as a child and teenager, discovering yet another aspect of him that wove silken bounds of shared experiences between them. Time flew by, and when she glanced at her watch and realized how late it was, she was shocked.

"Oh, Trace, it's nearly midnight!" She jumped down from the stool and caught up her discarded jacket from the polished hood of the Chevy. "I'm so sorry, I didn't mean to keep you from your work!"

"Hey, don't worry about it." Trace would have gladly spent until dawn talking to her. She seemed to relax more with him with each conversation, open up more, and unconsciously confide details about herself that gave him glimpses of her that he found endlessly fascinating. "I'll follow you home."

"No, absolutely not," Lily said with determination. "It's bad enough that I've kept you from your work this long."

Much as he argued, she was adamant and he finally, reluctantly, gave in, but not without extracting a promise that she'd call as soon as she reached home.

He stood in the shop's doorway and watched her hurry across the street, ducking her head against the wind that had sprung up while she'd been inside, and he stayed there until she disappeared down the block and around the corner. He knew a surge of rejection that he had to let her go home alone. He wanted to go with her, follow her into the bedroom, and tumble her onto the soft mattress.

He sighed, shoved his fingers through tousled hair, and closed the outer door against the cold and wind to return to the waiting '49 Chevy.

# SIX

"Trace, I'm not sure about this." Lily's steps lagged as they walked up the sidewalk to his parents' home.

"Why?" He looked down at her, lifting a questioning brow at the worried expression on her delicate face.

"Isn't this a family gathering? I don't want to intrude."

"Intrude? You've got to be kidding." It had taken him fifteen minutes to talk her into spending the afternoon with him; Trace wasn't about to let her back out now. "There's no way of knowing who'll show up at my mom and dad's on Saturday afternoon. One more person more or less won't phase my mom."

"Are you sure?" She inspected his handsome face for honesty and found only directness in his blue gaze.

"I'm sure." Trace fought down the need to kiss her that was growing daily more insistent. "You'll probably know everybody here. So stop worrying."

He pulled open the front door and stood back to let Lily enter first. She stepped across the threshold and, as always, was swept with a feeling of welcome, generated by the scent of furniture polish, the savory smells of cooking emanating from the kitchen down the long hall directly in front of them, and the sounds of laughter from the parlor that opened off the entryway to their left. Trace took her coat and hung it next to his on a hook on the antique coat rack.

"Come on, we'll say hi to Mom first." He ushered her ahead of him down the hallway and into the kitchen.

Jeannie McFadden was standing at the stove, stirring the contents of a steaming kettle.

"Hi, Mom." Trace crossed the room and dropped a kiss on her cheek.

Jeannie smiled up at her tall son.

"Hi, yourself." She glanced across the room and her smile widened as she saw Lily. "Hello, Lily, I'm so glad you could make it today. Trace told me that he was going to try to talk you into joining us."

"Are you sure you have room for me?" Lily asked, although Jeannie's easy warmth had nearly erased any concern she had about being welcome.

"Heavens, yes! We always have room for one more. I never know who'll show up on Saturday afternoon, so I always cook enough for a mob."

"It's a good thing," Trace commented, reaching behind her to dip a spoon into the chili she was stirring. "I'm starved."

"You're always starved." Jeannie rapped his knuckles with her wooden spoon handle and he winced, but still managed to reach his mouth with the chili. "Scram out of my kitchen!"

"Yes, ma'am," he said meekly, eyes twinkling, and paused long enough to grab two sodas from the refrigerator before leading Lily back down the hall to the parlor.

"Hey, Trace." Mike Hoffman, a football fan from across the street, greeted them with enthusiasm. "You want to bet on the game?"

"Sure, I get the Hawkeyes," Trace answered, taking Lily's arm to steer her to a high-backed, overstuffed armchair in the corner.

"All right," Mike grumbled. "Two bucks on the Hawkeyes."

"Has everybody here met Lily?" Trace asked, raising his voice over the sound of the crowd cheers and the sportscaster on television.

"Yeah. Hi, Lily."

"Of course. Hi, Lily."

The friendly hellos echoed from the seven people seated around the room and Trace gently pushed Lily into the chair and dropped onto the floor in front of her, leaning his back against the seat. His shoulder snugged against her leg, his body warmth penetrating through his gray sweater and her red wool slacks to her skin.

Lily determinedly ignored the feel of his arm and shoulder against her leg and concentrated on the football game. Football wasn't something she watched normally, but the group in the parlor were such enthusiastic, diehard fans that their excitement was contagious, and by halftime, she found herself cheering and groaning at the plays with as much enthusiasm as Trace.

"Halftime," Trace said, glancing up at her flushed face. "Time for a break."

He stood and caught her hand to pull her up out of the chair.

Lily felt the familiar tingle when his calloused palm and fingers closed around her softer hand. He didn't touch her often, but when he did, she always felt that same pleasurable shiver of awareness that carried an odd sense of déjà vu and made her wonder if the pleasure would increase if she allowed him closer. He didn't push, however, releasing her hand as soon as she was standing, and she didn't have the courage to explore the possibility by clinging to his fingers.

"Where are we going?" she asked as he led her out into the hall.

"Upstairs. I want to show you something."

Obediently, she followed his broad back as he climbed the blue-carpeted wide stairs to the second floor and down the wide hall. He pushed open a door and stood back to let her enter.

"Whose room is this?" she asked, her gaze taking in the two twin beds and braided wool rugs, the walls nearly covered with posters, pennants, pictures of cars and ribbons and awards.

"Nobody's, now," Trace answered, his hands shoved deep in his pockets as he stood in the center of the rug and looked around the room. "It was mine and Cole's before we left home."

"Oh." Filled with curiosity, Lily walked farther into the room. Snapshots were tucked into the frame around a mirror and she leaned closer to inspect them. A young, teenage Trace grinned back at her from black-and-white and colored photos, and in several of them, he was accompanied by an older version of himself that she guessed must be the missing Cole. "You played football in high school?" she asked, gazing at a shot of Trace kneeling with a row of uniform-clad young men, all holding a helmet under their arm.

"Yeah." Trace moved to stand behind her. "I was a linebacker."

"I don't see any blood and bruises," Lily teased, smiling at him over her shoulder.

"That's because the picture was taken *before* the game," he responded, his grin flashing whitely.

"Ah, I see." Lily picked up a trophy from the top of the desk and read the inscription aloud. "Cole McFadden,

First Place, Spirit Lake Drag Strip. Did your brother always race cars, even in high school?"

"Cole raced cars since the day he was born," Trace responded. "I don't think there was ever a time when he wanted to do anything else."

"And did you always want to renovate classic cars?" she asked, smoothing her fingertips over the miniature metal car crowning the trophy she held.

"From about the seventh grade on, I did. That's what comes of having a dad who lives and breathes cars and engines; we spent a lot of time with Dad down at his shop while we were growing up. He builds engines for race car owners from all over the United States, and when they were in town, Dad usually brought them here to stay, so we not only were influenced by Dad, but by most of the big names in racing."

"So you all chose careers connected to racing or cars," Lily said, watching his face, his gaze intent as he talked about his profession.

"Except for Josh." Trace's blue eyes lit with affection. "He's the rebel among us. He works for the Department of Immigration, and even when he was a kid, he refused to drive a nice car. He drove the worst pieces of junk I've ever seen and the only halfway nice vehicle he ever owned was a chopped Harley Davidson motorcycle. Dad told him he looked like a Hell's Angel. Dad's not crazy about motorcycles," he added wryly, and was rewarded by Lily's laughter.

She returned the trophy to the desktop.

"So," she said, her gaze wandering over the memorabilia that filled the room. "What was it you wanted to show me?"

"This . . ." He crossed the room and knelt in front of a walnut bookcase. "Come here," he urged, beckoning to her.

Curious, she obeyed his crooked finger and went to him, kneeling beside him on the braided wool rug.

"Oh," she breathed softly as she ran a finger over the spines of the worn leather-bound books that filled the shelves. "All my favorites!" She glanced sideways at him through her lashes. "You weren't kidding, you really did read a lot." She looked back at the titles on the shelves. "Do you still spend a lot of time reading?"

"Not as much as I used to, but then I don't have as much free time as I did when I was in school. Mom gets advance copies from her publisher of new books by authors that she particularly likes and I read the ones that she says are too good to miss, but other than that, it's pretty much hit and miss."

Lily wondered again how he'd had time to earn the reputation with women that gossip credited him with, what with building his business and other pursuits. The Trace McFadden she was growing to know was far more complex than she'd guessed, far more attractive, and far more difficult to dismiss.

She looked up from her contemplation of the well-worn books to find Trace watching her with eyes that darkened from sapphire to navy-blue as they moved slowly over her face before fastening on her mouth. Lily couldn't move; she could only gaze helplessly as his head lowered slowly toward hers, her heart shuddering with equal parts anticipation, fear, and an odd sense that they'd done this before, as she waited with caught breath for his mouth to touch hers.

"Trace!" Jesse's voice echoed up the stairwell and penetrated the spell that held them. "Halftime's over!"

Trace swallowed a groan, and he froze, his mouth only a whisper from Lily's. Startled, her drowsy eyes opened wide and he read confusion and surprise in the lavender depths before she dropped concealing lashes and turned to replace the book she held on the shelf.

"We'd better go downstairs." Her usually husky tones were ragged and breathless. "You don't want to miss the game."

She stood quickly and left the room. Trace heaved a sigh and rose to follow her.

*If I could get my hands on Jesse, I'd kill him,* he thought with frustration. *What lousy timing!*

"I should never have let you take the Hawkeyes," Mike grumbled as he counted out two one-dollar bills into Trace's palm. "How about a little touch football? I need a shot at winning my two bucks back."

"I don't know, Mike." Trace glanced at Lily, who stood near the hall door talking to Gavin, a smile lighting her face as his dad said something Trace couldn't hear.

"Come on, Trace, what's the matter? Afraid we'll beat you?" Mike's wife teased, eyes twinkling as she looked up at her husband.

"Beat him at what?" Jesse asked, unfolding his long length from the sofa just in time to hear the comment.

"Mike and I are going to clobber Trace at touch football," DeeDee Hoffman said with relish.

"Uh-oh, a challenge! You hear that, Gavin, Mike and DeeDee are going to wipe us out!"

"Hey, wait a minute!" Mike protested. "We're not taking you all on. We have to split into teams, there's too many of you and only two of us."

"All right," Jesse said. "You get Lily and Gavin, and Sarah and I will play on Trace's team."

Trace caught the quick, brief flicker of panic across Lily's features.

"Nope, I get Lily, Mike can have Sarah."

In the ensuing bickering over who was playing on what

team, Trace left the group and stepped over floor pillows and around chairs to reach Lily. His heart lurched at the worry in the lavender eyes turned up to his.

"Trace," she whispered. "I don't know about this—I've never played football."

Trace smiled reassuringly, registering her instinctive, protective withdrawal.

"You don't have to know much, honey. This is touch football. That means no tackling, and no rough stuff. To tackle somebody, the opposing player has to touch the ball carrier with two hands below the waist."

She still wasn't sure if she wanted to play, and her gaze went past him to the friendly wrangling going on behind his shoulder as the group settled who was playing on what team. They were all friendly, nice people, and she didn't want to offend them, but she instinctively shied away from becoming involved in a situation she wasn't familiar with. Long ago, she'd learned the best way to protect herself was to move within known parameters.

"You'll be on my team and I promise I'll do my best to keep them from touching you," Trace promised, seeing the uncertainty clearly visible on her face as she looked past him to the friendly group. His heart ached at the inbred, wary caution with which she faced each new situation. "Come on, honey, you'll have fun, trust me."

*Trust me.* Lily's gaze moved back to Trace and she realized with a start of surprise that she did trust him. It was such a shocking revelation that she could only stare at him.

"Come on, Trace." The group behind him split up and moved toward the door. "You've got Lily, Jesse, Bruce, and Trisha on your team."

"Okay, fine," he answered absentmindedly, unable to pull his gaze away from Lily's. He'd become adept at reading her thoughts from her expressive face, but she was staring at him now with arrested surprise, lavender eyes fastened on his with a searching intensity that baffled him. "Lily . . ." he said tentatively, and was rewarded with a quick return of awareness on her delicate features.

The crowd surged past them and out into the hall.

"All right," she told him with calm sureness, "but if I wind up covered with dirt and bruises, I'm going to hold you *personally* responsible!"

Trace didn't know what had tipped the scales in his favor, but he shot a quick silent *thank you* skyward as he followed her slim figure in red slacks and sweater outside.

Mike already had his team in a huddle when Trace and Lily reached the neighborhood park a short few blocks away. They jogged across the neatly trimmed grass, spattered with the last few red-and-gold leaves from the massive oaks that lined the sidewalks and joined Jesse's huddle.

"Who's quarterbacking, Trace, you or me?" Jesse asked.

"Me," Trace answered promptly, grinning at Jesse's grimace.

"All right, but after the first five points, we switch," Jesse said in a no-nonsense voice.

"Sounds good." Trace's glance moved around the circle of faces and found several that hadn't been at his dad's house. "I see we've picked up a few team members." The grinning faces of two teenage boys and a neighborhood girl looked back at him. "Samantha, are you sure you want to play with these guys? They might get rough."

"I'm sure," the wiry little ten-year-old said stoutly.

"I thought you told me that nobody got tackled and this *wouldn't* get rough?" Lily said quickly, shooting Trace a suspicious glance.

"It won't, it won't, not with you, I promise," Trace

assured her. "But I can't watch both you and Samantha at the same time."

"I'll look out for Samantha," Jesse declared, winking at the little girl who gave him a cocky grin in return.

"And we'll look out for Trisha!" the two young teenage boys chimed in, eliciting a groan from Mike and DeeDee's curvy, older teenage daughter.

"Just be sure you remember that you're *not* supposed to tackle me!" she warned them.

"Here's the plan," Trace said, demanding their attention. "Chuck, you snap the ball. Jesse, you split out to the right and run a deep post; if you're open, I'll get the ball to you. Samantha, I want you to split out to the left, go down five yards and break over the middle. If Jesse can't get open, I'll drop it off to you. I want you to line up to my left, Lily. If nobody gets open, I'll hand you the ball and you'll run a sweep to the right side. Just stay behind me and I'll block for you. The rest of you line up and block." He ran an inspecting glance around the circle of attentive faces. "Everybody got that? Any questions? Good. Snap it on two, Chuck, and let's see some good blocking up there!"

The huddle broke up with yells and cheers and re-formed in a rough pattern on the grass across from Mike's team.

"What do we do if Jesse catches the ball?" Lily asked Trace as she lined up several yards away on his left.

"Then you run down the field yelling." Trace grinned, anticipation of the coming battle gleaming in his blue eyes.

"What good does that do?" she asked, perplexed.

"Absolutely none, but it's fun! Not to mention great exercise."

"Hey, Trace! You ready back there?" Chuck yelled, viewing the brawny quarterback and his lady upside down from between his legs while he waited to snap the ball.

Trace's attention switched back to the game and he stood half-crouched behind his center, looking right and left to check the team's position.

"Heads up, guys!" he called. "Hut-one, hut-two."

Chuck snapped the ball into his waiting hands, and Trace took two steps back. All around him was pandemonium as the opposing team ran to tackle him. Jesse ran his pattern with the surefooted ease of long practice and Trace threw the football with unerring accuracy into his waiting hands. Jesse tucked it under his arm and ran, fleet-footed, toward the goal.

The focus of the teams shifted from the quarterback to the ball carrier and they switched direction to chase him. Lily found herself caught up in the excitement and ran with everyone else, until Jesse crossed the goal line.

"Touchdown!" He held his arms up in victory.

After much good-natured grumbling, the two teams regrouped in the center of the field. This time it was Mike's team's turn to hike the ball, and they, too, ran it down the field for a touchdown.

"We'll run the same play," Trace told his team. "Snap it on two, Chuck."

This time, Mike's team was ready for them and Trace found no open pass receivers, both Jesse and Samantha were surrounded.

"Okay, Lily, here we go." He passed the ball to her and barely took time to notice her tuck it close to her body before he took off down the field.

It happened so fast, Lily didn't have time to be nervous. She hugged the ball against her ribs and followed Trace's fast-moving figure; dodging and weaving, she ran the length of the grassy field. Just when she thought she was home free, two opposing players converged on her and Sarah tagged her.

"Just follow me." She mimicked Trace's deep voice as

she laughed up at him. "I thought you said you were going to run interference for me?"

Flushed and disheveled, her cheeks rivaling the red of her sweater, lavender eyes sparkling with elation, she was so gut-wrenchingly lovely that it was all Trace could do not to sweep her up into a bone-crushing hug.

"I said I wouldn't let you get tackled and bruised," he corrected her. "Is it my fault that you strolled down the field instead of running?"

"Strolled!?" Her thick lashes narrowed over lavender eyes, threatening retribution. "I'll show you strolled! Next time we do this, you better pray I don't run right up your back."

"Promises, promises," he laughed, and dodged the blow she aimed at his shoulder.

"Hey, you two," Gavin called. "You're supposed to beat the other team, not each other!"

"Yeah, let's play ball," Chuck yelled.

The next three plays netted neither team additional points. Then Samantha carried the football over the goal line for a touchdown, beaming with pride when Trace picked her up and carried her back up the field on his shoulders to the cheers of the other team members.

Mike's team, determined to score, made a touchdown, and then another, until the game was tied.

"Come on, you guys," Trace said. "I've got two bucks riding on this game! We need another touchdown!"

"You get the ball to me, I'll get you a touchdown," Jesse said, and the teams lined up again.

"Hut-one, hut-two." Chuck snapped the ball and Trace dropped back to throw, but Mike's team had Jesse and Samantha well covered, and with no receivers open, once again he handed the ball off to Lily.

"Come on, sweetheart," he yelled, blue eyes gleaming. "Run!"

Lily tucked the ball into her ribs and ran. But by now the opposition knew what to expect and they converged on her like a swarm of locusts.

Trace glanced over his shoulder and saw Mike, Gavin, and Sarah all honing in on Lily's running figure. With a jolt, he realized that they were all going to reach the same point on the playing field at the same time and there was no way in hell that they could keep from colliding.

He switched directions to intercept them and plucked Lily out of the midst of the three a bare second before the trio went down in a tangle of rolling bodies and pinwheeling arms and legs. But his quick action cost him his balance and he fell, instinctively wrapping his arms around her slim body and rolling so that he hit the ground first, with Lily on top of him.

Stunned, he opened his eyes and looked up to find her wide-eyed and startled, the football an uncomfortable leather lump that she clutched between them. Her surprise faded into amusement, and she laughed down at him, her slim body shaking with giggles as he tried to catch his breath.

"You didn't tell me you were going to keep me from getting bruises by throwing your body down beneath mine," she teased around fits of giggles as he drew in deep gasps in an effort to get his breath. "You're a regular Sir Galahad."

"Jeez, woman," he complained. "If I'd known how much you weigh, I'd never have done it!"

"Hah," she sniffed, eyes sparkling. "I'll bet Sir Galahad never complained."

"Only because he never had to play touch football with you," he returned promptly. His arms loosened immediately when she wiggled and he hid his disappointment when she rolled to her feet.

"Sarah, are you all right?" Lily called.

Trace lay spreadeagled and flat on his back, turning his head sideways against the cool grass to watch her walk over to his sister and the two men, who were laughing and getting to their feet, brushing off grass and twigs, while the remaining members of the two teams circled them.

*Damn,* he thought wistfully. *The first time I get to hold her, and we have to be surrounded by a dozen people.*

A fist pounded loudly on Lily's front door, rattling the wooden panels. Reading glasses perched on the end of her nose, she looked up from the student papers she was nearly finished grading and glanced at the clock on top of the little portable television.

*Who can that be at this hour? It's nearly ten o'clock,* she mused. Trace was out of town in South Carolina, helping his brother Cole with something on his race car. He'd explained what he was doing, but for Lily, he might as well have been speaking Japanese. He wasn't due back until tomorrow. She shifted the notebook and sheaf of papers off her lap and onto the sofa cushion and padded in stocking feet across the floor to flip on the porch light and peer through the curtain.

A smile of delight burst across her face and she quickly slipped the locks and pulled open the door.

"Trace! What are you doing here? I thought you weren't coming back until tomorrow?"

She held the door wide and stepped back to let him inside, shivering with the cold draft of air that entered with him.

"I caught an earlier plane home after I heard the weather report."

"Weather report?"

"Yeah—you mean you don't know?"

"Know what?" she asked, looking at him in bewilderment.

"Snow! It's the first snow of the year!"

Lily looked at him, really looked, and blinked slowly as she realized that his brown leather bomber jacket was dusted with melting flakes of snow and white prisms were caught in his hair and even on his lashes. She flushed, realizing that she'd been so glad to see him that all she'd registered was the surge of pure pleasure that he was home early.

"Oh," she said stupidly, her brain still not caught up with her emotions.

Trace hadn't missed the flash of welcoming delight that lit her violet eyes and curved her mouth when she opened the door to him. He wanted nothing more than to pull her against him and kiss her senseless; he'd missed her unbearably in the last five days, and from the look on her face, she hadn't enjoyed their separation, either. He stuffed his hands into his jacket pockets to keep them from reaching out and grabbing her.

"Yeah, oh, snow—so get your jacket and boots and gloves and scarf and let's go."

"Go? Go where?"

"Earth to Lily, Earth to Lily," Trace said in a monotone and waved a testing hand in front of her eyes. With a familiar ease that would have been impossible weeks before, she reached up and swatted his hand away.

"Where are you dragging me this time?" she demanded, propping her hands on her hips.

"Outside, where else?" His eyes sparkled with excitement. "It's snowing, Lily! The first snow of the season, and it's beautiful. Come on, don't be such a wimp. It's really not that cold out there."

"Hah," she said grumpily. "That's what you always say!" But she pulled her scarlet wool jacket out of the closet and tugged on her boots. Trace waited impatiently while she found her white fur earmuffs and gloves and wound a matching scarf around her throat.

"It's about time," he complained goodnaturedly. "Women!" He rolled his eyes skyward and adroitly avoided the punch she aimed at his shoulder. "Come on, come on."

He pulled her outside and down the sidewalk to the street.

There was no wind and the snow fell silently earthward from the dark sky in a straight line, blanketing the world with white and turning the familiar boulevard into frosted beauty.

Trace tucked her hand into the bend of his arm and shoved his hands into his pockets. They walked silently, entranced by the winter wonderland they walked through. The snow was dry and powdery and their feet scuffed through it, kicking it up to cling to the legs of their jeans. There was no traffic and Trace led her down the middle of the street until they turned the corner onto Hill Avenue. Here the wide avenue was bisected lengthwise by planting strips that in summer were long oases of green grass and towering oaks that threw shade across the pavement on either side. But now the dried grass was hidden beneath a covering of soft white snow and the tall oaks lifted bare, skeletal arms toward the night sky, their trunks sturdy black shapes against the falling white curtain.

They walked for a long time, speaking rarely and then in hushed tones, awed by the silent arrival of winter's beauty. The old-fashioned city lampposts created pools of golden light that illuminated the silent fall of white flakes. Trace and Lily walked in and out of the pools of light and darkness until Trace slowed to a halt beneath the glow of one of the old carved iron posts.

Lily tilted her face up to his, and her breath caught in

his throat. Snow continued to fall softly around them, frosting her hair and catching on the tips of her lashes, her cheeks reddened with cold. But it was her eyes that melted his heart and sent a surge of fierce emotion rushing through his veins. Those violet eyes held the enchanted glow of a child's and all the awe and wonder that echoed in his own heart at the sight of God's handiwork that surrounded them.

"Lily," he managed to get out hoarsely, and he lifted a hand to brush the backs of trembling fingers against her cheek. He swallowed jerkily, so afraid that he didn't know the right words. "I badly need to kiss you. Do you think maybe you're ready to let me?"

Lily gazed silently up into his handsome face, a face that had somehow become dear to her heart. So slowly that she'd hardly realized that it was happening, his had become the face that she looked for in every crowd, that she waited for to appear at her door, and that she'd missed more than she had thought possible over the last five days. And Lily realized that the impossible had happened. She wanted to kiss him. She was still afraid, but the need to satisfy her own curiosity, and the need and desire to give him what he so clearly wanted, was stronger than her fear.

Still, her voice trembled with apprehension when she answered him.

"Yes," she said softly, her gaze fastened on his. "Yes. I think I'm ready."

The hand against her cheek jerked in reaction. His other hand, deep in his pocket, unconsciously tightened into a fist, and the muscles of his forearm flexed, pressing their looped arms tightly against his ribs.

"Thank you, God," he murmured fervently, *and please don't let me screw this up*.

His fingers moved against her face, cradling the soft, delicate bones of cheek and jaw in his palm and fingers.

His other hand stayed clenched in his pocket; he was afraid to hold her for fear that he'd scare her. Carefully, he bent his head and touched his lips to hers in a tentative, gentle tasting. The kiss was almost chaste, closed mouth moving slowly against soft, closed mouth, but it was all of heaven and hell for Trace. The satiny skin of her cheek was cold against his nose, but her mouth warmed beneath his, her lips moving in shy response.

Lily held her breath as Trace bent toward her, her body stiffening as if preparing for an assault. But he didn't try to hold her, and his hand stayed on her face, cradling her cheek in his warm palm and calloused fingers. When his lips touched hers, she jerked slightly in reaction, but when his mouth didn't grind painfully against hers but, instead, brushed her lips with soft, tasting movements, she forgot to worry and began to enjoy. When at last he reluctantly lifted his head and looked down at her, she was breathing faster, her body heated, the cold weather forgotten.

Trace's own breathing was labored, his body singing with the hot blood that surged through his veins, swelling his body with a fierce, urgent need that he hadn't felt since high school.

*My God,* he thought with awe. *And I only kissed her!*

# SEVEN

Lily's lashes lifted slowly and the violet gaze that met his was soft and unfocused, dazed with pleasure.

''Oh, my goodness,'' she murmured, releasing caught breath in a soft sigh. The calloused fingers moving against her cheek with gentle strokes held a faint tremor and she resisted the urge to turn her face into his warm palm.

''Are you all right?'' he asked unsteadily, his gaze searching her upturned face.

''I'm fine,'' she whispered, and a small shaky smile curved her mouth.

Trace swallowed jerkily, and the tense worry that strung his body relaxed. With an effort, he forced reluctant fingers to leave the soft, warm silkiness of her cheek and brushed her hair back over her shoulder. The thick strands were cold and dampened with snow.

''I'd better get you home,'' he said huskily. ''You're going to catch pneumonia.''

But he didn't move, he couldn't force himself to step away from her.

Lily realized that she was standing motionless, staring

up into his face while his hand continued to smooth over the damp thickness of her hair. With an effort, she forced her fingers to unclench their grip on the front of his jacket. She vaguely remembered catching the cold brown leather tightly to steady herself against a world that tipped on its axis to spin crazily, while skyrockets exploded when Trace's warm mouth moved against hers.

She took a small step back and his hand slid reluctantly from her hair.

His fist unclenched inside his pocket and he caught her gloved fingers, threading his own through hers before tucking their joined hands back into his jacket pocket. She didn't protest and they walked quietly through the falling snow, their bodies touching only in the warm, snug clasp of hands. By the time they reached her house and climbed the porch steps, their cheeks and noses were pink with cold, their toes chilled inside their boots.

Trace held open her screen door while she fumbled in her coat pocket and found the key to unlock her front door.

Lily had grown increasingly nervous on the walk back, wondering if he would assume that she'd ask him to come inside. She wanted more kisses, but she wasn't sure she was ready to deal with him alone in the house, without the restraints of coats and cold snow.

She fumbled with the key, and Trace took it from her numb fingers, twisting it in the metal lock before pushing the door inward. She tugged on their clasped hands and Trace let her retrieve her hand from his pocket, but refused to unthread his fingers from hers. She stepped across the threshold and turned to look up at him.

Trace read the uncertainty on her face and lifted his free hand to smooth the worried little frown from between her brows.

"Stop that," he ordered softly, a small smile lifting the

corners of his mouth. "I'm not going to jump your bones, and I'm not going to ask you to let me come in. We aren't going to do anything that you don't want to and I'm not going to make any demands, okay?"

"Okay." Lily nodded, unable to conceal the flood of relief that filled her.

"All you have to do is say no." Trace's hand lingered, his forefinger tracing the arch of her brow and moving slowly over the smooth skin of cheekbone and cheek before finding the corner of her mouth. His thumb slid slowly over her lower lip, pressing gently. Lily's lips parted in unconscious, natural response and his heart shuddered against his ribs. He drew a deep breath and tried to slow down. "Of course, the rules don't apply to you. You can do anything you want to me." His blue gaze left its intent appraisal of her mouth and flicked back up to meet hers. "Wouldn't you like to kiss me good night?"

Lily's heart lurched at the hungry need in the blue eyes and her throat went dry.

"Yes," she whispered, and was rewarded with an instant flare of response in the depths of his eyes. "Please."

He bent toward her and this time there was no flinching as she trustingly lifted her mouth to meet his. Their bodies only touched at clasped hands and warm mouths, but by the time Trace slowly lifted his head, her lips clung, following his, reluctant to let him go. He tugged gently on her hand and she took a small step forward, stopping just short of touching him. His face only inches above hers, he watched the emotion flickering in her violet eyes and across her expressive features while he slowly slid his arms around her. A brief flare of panic surged in her lavender gaze, but when he left the circle of his arms loose and didn't force her closer, the panic receded, replaced by anticipation.

Trace obeyed the silent invitation when she tilted her face up to his and kissed her again, brief, tasting kisses against the corner of her mouth, her cheek, the frantically beating pulse at her temples, before returning to her mouth.

The long, slow kiss had their hearts shuddering and temperatures climbing, and by the time Trace eased the warm pressure of his mouth against hers, their breathing was labored, cheeks flushed with heat.

"I have to say good night," he said with husky effort. "God knows I don't want to—I could stay right here kissing you until the sun comes up, but I don't want you out in the cold any longer."

Lily thought dazedly that she would have willingly stood there kissing him until dawn and not minded at all, but his protective concern warmed her, gently healing old scars.

"Will I see you tomorrow?" she asked in a throaty murmur.

"Absolutely. Want to go to dinner?"

"I'd love to, but I have to work late; can you pick me up at school?"

"Sure." Trace brushed a kiss against her cheek. "What time?"

"Uhmm." Lily closed her eyes, distracted by his warm lips moving against her skin. "I should be through by six. I'm tutoring Kari after class."

"Okay," he murmured. Reluctantly, he forced his lips to leave the smooth warmth of her cheek and let his arms fall away from her. He stepped back, observing the warm, bemused look on her face with satisfaction. "Close the door," he said gently.

Lily took a small step back and caught the edge of the door.

"Good night," she said softly.

"Good night." Trace watched the door close away the sight of her flushed cheeks and well-kissed mouth and forced himself not to follow her. He waited until he heard the bolt shoot home before he closed the screen door and left the front porch.

Lily shed her clothes and donned a flannel nightgown in a daze, rubbing her hair dry with a towel that she left tossed on the bathroom cabinet in a damp pile. Completely unlike her usual fastidiousness, her snow-dampened jeans lay crumpled on the bathroom floor tiles, although she did remember to hang her wet coat and scarf up to dry.

She turned back the comforter and sheets on the brass bed and perched on the edge, staring at the fern by the window without really seeing the green fronds. Her hand pulled a brush through the tangled strands of her damp hair, smoothing it in hypnotic strokes while her mind relived every detail of the last hour.

The hand holding the brush fell unheeded into her lap while she relived Trace's mouth moving against hers. Far from the painful, unfulfilling encounters she'd grown accustomed to with Derek, she'd actually enjoyed the feel of his lips against hers. For the first time, she'd caught a glimpse of the pleasure a man and a woman can give each other. Even in the beginning of her brief marriage, before Derek had grown frustrated with her lack of response and experience and moved on to anger, violence, and other women, she'd never felt the jolt of pure heated wanting that ignited her with Trace.

*Wanting*. Unconsciously, she lifted her fingers to her lips. *I wanted him to kiss me*, she thought with amazement. *And I didn't get claustrophobic and panicky when he held me.*

Was it possible that with Trace, the intimacies of lovemaking might feel the way they looked between lovers in movies?

The chill of the bedroom penetrated the flannel of her gown and she shivered. The clock on her bedside table told her that it was well after midnight and, with a sigh, she snapped off the lamp and snuggled under the heavy comforter. Outside, the snow continued to fall, sifting through the branches of tree limbs and the bare twigs of bushes, shrouding the world in a thick white carpet. Inside, Lily tried without success to sleep, the events of the evening playing over and over in her mind.

*Would it be so terrible to take a chance with Trace?* she asked the silent ceiling. *He promised that we wouldn't do anything I don't want to do and that he wouldn't make any demands. So far, he's never been anything other than kind. He's absolutely nothing like Derek,* she realized with absolute surety. *But what if the problem wasn't Derek? What if I really am no good in bed and what happened between us wasn't Derek's fault, but mine?* She pushed the thought from her mind. If there was one thing she'd learned in counseling, it was that even if she wasn't good at sex, Derek hadn't been entitled to hit her. So the real question was, if the reality was that Trace was as disappointed in her performance as Derek had been, would he react the way Derek had, with violence and abuse? Everything in her instinctively shouted no. Trace wasn't Derek.

The next question was, did she want to have an affair with Trace? The answer was an amazing, unequivocal yes.

Lily was astounded at herself. She knew very well that Trace loved women and that to him, she was just another romantic interlude until he moved on to the next pretty face. Trace McFadden was a man who would never be interested in marriage and she was a woman who could never have forever. Painfully, she faced the fact that when their affair ended, it would break her heart. But in the meantime, surely God wouldn't judge her too harshly for taking a bit of happiness to hold against the long, lonely years ahead.

Deciding to let events proceed at the slow, easy pace Trace had already set, Lily stifled a yawn and closed her eyes. Sleep welcomed her, and the music moving rhythmically through her dreams waited to catch her with loving, open arms, while a contented, happy smile curved her mouth.

Trace walked down the hallway of West High the following evening at a quarter to six. Lily wasn't in the big band room with its semicircle of chairs and music stands, so he kept going, following the muffled sound of a piano. The small practice rooms that lined the hallway had large, square windows in their doors and Trace soon located Lily. When he eased the door open, music poured out, flooding the hallway until he stepped inside and let the door close silently behind him.

Lily sat with her back to him, her long hair flowing over her shoulders, black strands catching against her jacket. The sleeves of her lavender wool suit jacket were rolled up to make cuffs, exposing the violet silk lining and the long sleeves of the white cotton turtleneck she wore beneath. The overhead light caught the glint of a silver ring as her fingers moved over the ivory keys of a scarred practice piano. The small room was filled with the music; Trace could almost touch the notes that rippled and flowed in the air, swooping and soaring on wings of sound. He didn't recognize the melody, he didn't think he'd ever heard it before, but the emotions that the music stirred were very familiar. The music suddenly ceased in mid bar and he felt a quick, intense sense of loss. Lily stood and turned away from the bench, and her eyes widened with welcome, a smile lighting her face.

"Don't stop," he said quickly. "Finish it."

"It doesn't have a finish," she laughed self-consciously. "Actually, it doesn't even have a beginning."

"Why not?"

"Because it isn't a song. I was just fooling around."

"You mean, you were making that up as you went along?" Trace's eyes widened.

Lily shrugged and turned her back to close the lid over the keys.

"Lily, that was great." Trace saw the slight stiffening of her shoulders and his long strides shortened the distance between them to a few feet. "You don't like hearing that your music is wonderful?" he asked, confused by her reaction.

"It's not that." Lily turned to face him. Tears misted her eyes and her mouth trembled.

"Hey . . ." Trace cupped her cheek in a hard palm, worried dread swamping him. "What's wrong? Why are you crying?"

"Nothing's wrong." A smile broke across her face even as she lifted shaky fingertips to wipe away a tear that had escaped to roll down her cheek.

"Then why are you crying?" Trace asked, perplexed.

"Because it's been so long . . ." She paused, swallowing past the emotion that clogged her throat. "It's been so long since I've been able to do that."

"Do what? Play the piano?"

"No, I never stopped playing the piano, but for the last five years, the music stopped playing." Lily could tell by the expression on his face that he didn't understand, so she tried again. "It's difficult to explain, but ever since I was little—for as long as I can remember, really—music always played inside my head. Beginnings of songs, endings of songs, sometimes whole songs—but it was always there. Then, some," she faltered, and drew a deep breath before she could continue. "Some—bad—things happened in my life and I stopped hearing the music. But since I came to CastleRock and met you, I've started hearing the music again."

Trace looked down into her beloved, earnest face and felt a swelling of emotion that shook him. He smoothed his hand over the crown of her head and pulled her against him in a hug. At first she stiffened in reaction, then relaxed in his arms, her own arms tentatively circling his waist to hold him.

Trace buried his face in the scented silk of her hair and drew a deep breath.

"I'm glad, honey," he said huskily. "I'm really glad."

Lily moved through the next few weeks in a daze. Trace showered her with affection, and his constant touching became something she no longer feared, but instead, contact that she craved. He often pulled her against him for quick, spontaneous hugs and, gradually, her instinctive bracing stopped and she no longer flinched and panicked at being held within the circle of his arms. Although he dropped little kisses on her face often, he only kissed her, *really* kissed her, hello and good night. Lily found herself looking forward to those heated, soul-destroying meetings of their mouths with simmering anticipation and aching, unsatisfied need when Trace reluctantly forced himself to take his mouth and arms away from her.

"Come on, Lily, don't be such a chicken!"

Lily eyed Trace's sparkling eyes and bundled-up body with suspicion before peering down the long length of the toboggan slide. The high wooden structure, built on a hill that sloped abruptly to the frozen lakeshore, looked sturdy enough. But the shrieks of the toboggan riders as they hurtled down the slide and shot out over the frozen lake were long, loud, and, to Lily's apprehensive ears, slightly hysterical.

"Are you sure this is safe?" she asked dubiously.

"Of course it's safe! I've been tobogganing on this slide ever since I was a kid—Mom and Dad used to bring us to the slide every winter as soon as the lake was frozen solid. Dad even coaxed my mom to go down with him, and she loved it. He couldn't get out of the house without her after that; she always insisted on going with us."

"Hmm." Lily was unconvinced, but she allowed him to tug her forward.

Trace straddled the toboggan and looked up at her.

"Come on, sit down behind me. That's right . . ." He caught her ankles, hidden in thick boots, and tucked them close against the outside of his long legs. "Now put your hands around my waist."

Lily did so with trepidation, her heart leaping to lodge in her throat as he pushed off and the toboggan began to gain momentum.

"Wait!" she cried in panic. "I've changed my mind! I don't want to do this!"

"Too late!" he yelled over his shoulder, just as the toboggan teetered and tipped over the edge.

Lily screamed and buried her face in the back of his jacket, her mittened hands clutching fistfuls of his coat while her arms squeezed tightly. Cold wind stirred by their flight whipped past her face, and she narrowed her eyes over the tears it drew. The toboggan rocked, the wooden bottom rumbling over the ice-covered slide as they shot downward, the pitch of the slide making the sled pick up speed that sent them shooting off across the frozen surface of the lake.

They gradually lost speed and Lily loosed her death grip on Trace, laughing with exhilaration as they slowed.

Trace steered the toboggan between the banks of snow

until they came to a stop. He looked back over his shoulder and grinned at Lily's pink cheeks and laughing eyes.

"Still sure you don't want to do this?" he asked.

"No! It's great, just like riding a rocket!" She jumped up and tugged the steering rope out of his hands. "Come on, come on! Let's do it again!"

"Jeez," he groused, rolling to his feet. "You're just like my mother! I should never have started this!" He laughed, dodging the fist Lily aimed at his shoulder. "All right, all right, come on, we'll do it again."

They trudged off across the cleared ice, stopping to watch Sarah and Jesse as they careened out across the ice, miscalculated, and upended into a pile of snow. Lily's brief concern was quickly put to rest by the roar of laughter from the two as they stood and brushed off the snow.

"Nice move, Jesse," Trace called, laughing and ducking when Jesse threw a snowball at him that missed by a mile.

Lily was hooked. The foursome stood in line again and again, stamping cold feet to warm them while they waited for their turn on the slide.

"Let me steer this time, Trace," she coaxed, watching Trace line up the toboggan.

"All right." He held the sled while she sat down and wriggled herself into position before wedging himself behind her. With his long legs stretched out beside hers and his hard chest snugged against her back, Lily was surrounded by him, but she was having so much fun, she forgot to be frightened. He wrapped his arms around her and bent his head forward to growl threateningly in her ear, "Just don't steer us into a snowbank!"

"I can drive this thing," she assured him, then caught her breath as he pushed off and they started down the slide.

She didn't have Trace's broad back to shelter against,

and the cold wind hit her squarely in the face. She squealed and squinted her eyes nearly shut to protect them, but when the toboggan hit the ice, powdery snow sprayed upward and blinded her. She heard Trace yell something in her ear, but before she had time to respond, the front end of the toboggan climbed a bank of snow and rolled, tipping its riders off into the cold white powder.

Trace held on to Lily, cushioning her as their momentum sent them tumbling and rolling until they came to rest with him flat on his back and Lily stretched out on top of him, locked safely in his arms.

For a moment he just lay there, out of breath.

"That was fun! Let's do it again!"

He looked up to find Lily laughing down at him. She'd lost her tasseled, red knit ski cap and her hair tumbled around her face, her eyes gleaming with excitement and joy.

"I thought I told you not to steer us into a snowbank!" he growled with mock ferocity.

"I didn't do it on purpose. I couldn't see where I was going. Besides, the landing wasn't too bad, was it?"

"Not for you! You wound up on top."

Both were instantly, hotly, reminded of their position. Lily's legs were aligned with his, her hips pressed intimately against his and locked there by the circle of his arms. Despite the layers of wool that separated their bodies, each of them was desperately aware of the furnace heat of blood, muscle, and bone they lay against.

Trace's hand moved slowly up her back and into her hair, slowly closing into a fist, trapping strands of black silk.

"Lily," he said hoarsely, his gaze fastened intently on her face only inches above his own. "Kiss me." He'd kissed her often in the many nights since that eventful first snow of the season, but he desperately wanted her to initiate the joining.

To his shock and surprise, she only hesitated a moment before she lowered her face to his. Tentative and searching, she moved her lips against his. She'd learned a lot in those slow, torrid hello and good-night kisses they'd been sharing, and Trace was soon aroused and hot, too hot to remember that she was lying on top of him and he couldn't disguise his body's response.

But Lily was too aroused to be frightened and her own body responded in natural, seductive movements that sent Trace's temperature shooting higher. He endured the exquisite torture for as long as he could stand it before he caught her hips under the hard bar of his arm, one hand closing over her hipbone to hold her still, and tore his mouth from hers.

She dropped her face against the warmth of his neck, breathless.

Trace's breathing was fast and harsh against her temples, and even through the layers of jackets and sweaters, Lily could hear the thundering race of his heart.

"I think we better get up before we melt the ice," he managed to get out, his voice husky with arousal.

"All right," she whispered, reluctant to leave the hard body beneath her.

Tobogganing had lost its appeal. Trace and Lily were so vividly aware of each other that each successive ride down the long wooden slide, body snugged against body, was slow, teasing torture. Even sitting side by side in the little warming shack with its barrel stove, while they warmed frozen toes and noses and sipped hot chocolate, became a test in endurance. They withstood the sweet torment for an hour before they told Jessie and Sarah good night and left the frozen lake early.

Trace tugged Lily closer on the drive around the lake,

threading her fingers through his and holding them against the hard muscles of his thigh. He wanted her so badly he ached, and he looked forward to holding her and kissing her good night with an eagerness that was obsessive.

They reached her little house and Trace switched off the engine, pushed open the car door, and rounded the hood of the Camaro to pull open the passenger door for Lily. Silently, they walked up the snowy, shoveled sidewalk and climbed the porch steps. Still without speaking, he took the key from her hand and unlocked her front door.

With slow, deliberate movements, he tucked the key back into her pocket and lifted his gaze to hers. Her cheeks were already flushed with anticipation, her lashes half lowered over darkened lavender eyes that watched him with undisguised need. Trace slid his fingers into the thick silk of her hair and cradled her head, tugging her slowly forward to meet his descending mouth. Lily lifted her face willingly, and when their lips met, her small murmur of relief and pleasure echoed his needy groan. She snuggled closer and slid her arms around his waist.

When he finally lifted his mouth from hers, they were both flushed with heat, hearts shuddering.

"Ask me to come in," Trace murmured, his warm breath whispering against her lips, damp and slightly swollen from the long pressure of his.

Lily stared up into his face, reading the hot need in blue eyes.

"Come in," she said softly, and was rewarded by the leap of pure, undisguised pleasure that softened the hard lines of his face.

Trace's right hand reluctantly left her hair and fumbled behind her for the doorknob. The cold metal turned easily in his hand and he pushed the door inward. He walked

Lily backward the few steps necessary to enter the warm house and nudged the door shut with his elbow.

"Shouldn't we take our coats off?" Lily asked him breathlessly, having difficulty breathing when he trailed soft, open-mouthed kisses down her temple and along her jaw. Eyes drifting closed with pleasure, she tilted her head to allow him better access to the soft skin below her ear.

"Mmm," he mumbled in agreement, but it was several moments before he could force himself to leave the soft, scented skin.

Her arms left his waist and she took a small step back, pausing to flick the switch that turned on the lamp near the sofa. Trace shrugged out of his coat and tossed it over a chair seat. Lily was still fumbling with buttons and he stepped closer and brushed her hands aside.

"Here, let me," he said softly, a smile tugging up the corners of his mouth at her soft, still slightly unfocused violet eyes. He pushed the loosened coat off her shoulders and tossed it across the chair on top of his jacket before he tugged her gloves out of her hand and tossed them in the same general direction. "Come back here." He pulled her unresisting body back into his arms and returned to his exploration of her neck, nuzzling the scented silky mass of her hair that brushed against his face. Without taking his lips from her skin, he bent and slipped a hand under her knees to swing her up in his arms.

Lily gasped, her hands clutching his shoulders, and her eyes flew open.

"We're just going to sit down on the sofa," he said, his deep voice a husky murmur. "And we're not going to do anything you don't want to, okay?"

"Okay," she whispered, and promptly forgot her momentary unease when he hugged her close. She slid her fingers into the tawny thickness of his hair above the collar of his shirt and buried her face against his neck, inhaling the familiar scent of his aftershave.

Trace dropped onto the sofa cushions with Lily in his arms, and she nestled in his lap, curling closer when he wrapped his arms around her and returned his mouth to hers. Long moments passed and the slow movements of mouth against mouth grew hotter, until at last Trace released her to breathe. He was burning up and the feverish flush across Lily's cheeks told him she was, too.

"It's too hot in here," he muttered, brushing his thumb across her softly swollen lower lip before his fingers moved to the scarlet wool cardigan she wore and began to slip the buttons from their slots.

Lily didn't protest. It *was* too warm in the room, and she'd be much more comfortable in the cotton blouse she wore under the wool sweater. She refused to acknowledge that the prospect of fewer barriers between her skin and Trace's was irresistibly appealing. She lay against his shoulder and watched his face as he concentrated on buttons, his lashes half concealing the turbulence in his darkened blue eyes. She lifted a hand and traced the arch of a tawny brow and trailed fingertips across his cheekbone, marveling at the texture and heat of his skin before exploring the full curve of his lower lip. His lips parted and his tongue dampened the very tips of her fingers. Lily felt a surge of desire and, drawn irresistibly, turned his face to hers, tugging him down to replace her fingers with her mouth.

Trace's arms contracted to catch her against him, and his tongue traced the seam of her lips instead of her fingers. Lily obeyed the damp urging and opened her mouth to the exploration of his. Several long, steamy moments later, he forced his arms to loosen and he lifted his mouth from hers.

"It's your turn," he rasped, amazed that he could speak. "Take my sweater off."

Lily was having trouble breathing, let alone thinking, and it took her several, unblinking seconds to realize what he said. But when she did, she approved and pushed herself unsteadily upright. Tugging his sweater up his body was awkward while sitting sideways on his lap, so she got to her knees beside him and tugged. But that was awkward, too, and with an unthinking, trusting confidence that would have shocked her if she were in any condition to consider it, she straddled his lap, and with her knees securely bracing her against the sofa cushions, she pulled the cardigan up and off over his head. Trace cooperated, lifting his arms until she pulled the sweater free, emerging from the navy wool with tousled hair. She tossed the sweater aside and it landed against the sofa cushion before falling onto the carpet.

Trace smiled at the look of satisfied accomplishment on her face and slipped his arms around her to pull her against him. His mouth found hers with unerring precision and she sank willingly against him.

Totally absorbed in the heated magic of his mouth moving against hers, Lily wrapped her arms around his neck, flexing her fingers catlike against his shoulders, entranced by the hard, warm strength of the body she pressed against.

Trace doubted Lily was aware of the rhythmic brushing of her hips against his. But it was sending him nearly crazy with desire that pounded through his veins; he struggled to slow down, and failed.

Lily was hazily aware that he was unbuttoning her blouse, but felt only impatience until he brushed the material aside and his warm hands cupped her breasts. She gasped with surprise at the sheer force of the rivulets of pleasure that swelled her against his palms. His mouth released hers and she murmured a protest that quickly turned to catches of breath and sighs of pleasure when his lips brushed lower, lingering over her throat and the smooth, upper swell of her breasts until they explored the soft flesh barely concealed beneath the lace and satin of her bra. His hands moved over her back and the bra clasp gave way.

Trace smoothed his hands up her back and over the curve of her shoulders, taking the satin bra straps with him. Lily didn't object when he tugged blouse and bra free and let them fall to the floor. He trailed his fingers between the warm swell of her breasts before he moved to his own buttons. The back of his hand brushed against the satiny skin of her midriff and the velvety peaks of taut, full breasts as he yanked the buttons free and pushed his shirt aside, eliminating the last barrier between her skin and his.

"Lily," he groaned in near agony as he pulled her flush against him. Head to waist, they fit together, satiny skin sliding against sleek muscle.

Her bones turned to liquid heat, her body clinging to his when he moved, and she felt only satisfaction when she found herself stretched out on top of him on the sofa, the soft bareness of her shoulders, breasts, and midriff pressed against the smooth sleekness of hard muscles.

She lifted her head and looked down at him. His tawny hair was disheveled, his face flushed with heat, his blue eyes hot and dark as they held hers. She trailed fascinated fingers over the high thrust of his cheekbones and his jaw; splaying her hand wide just below his collarbone, she slowly pushed aside the edges of his shirt and smoothed her palms over the well-defined heavy muscles of his upper chest. To her delight, he reacted to her stroking hands with the same ripples and shudders of pleasure that wracked her when he touched her.

Trace struggled to hold on to his sanity. Her innocent, obviously fascinated exploration of his body was sweet torture. Tousled black hair fell around her shoulders like a satin cape and spilled forward to brush with silky, feathery strokes against his arms and chest each time she moved, creating a provocative shifting veil that revealed more than concealed rose-tipped breasts.

"Lily," he ground out, watching her through half-closed eyes, "you feel so damn good. I love your hands on me."

Lily felt a burst of pleasure. In the tide of desire that sucked her into a world bounded only by Trace and the intense pleasure he made her feel, she'd forgotten to worry about whether or not she was doing it right.

"Do you really?" she whispered, lavender eyes searching blue.

"Really," he whispered back, and slid his palm under her waistband to cup the smooth curve of her bottom. He pressed her closer, shifting his hips as he did. "Can't you tell?"

"Yes," she breathed, catching her breath at the blatant, powerful statement. His fingers moved, caressing the smooth skin in a rhythm that stroked the notch of her thighs against the heavy arousal straining the fabric that separated them. "Trace . . ." she began and paused, closing her eyes against the erotic surge of desire generated by the slow, torturous movements.

"What, baby?" Trace wanted this to go on forever, but he was afraid he was going to explode.

"I want to . . ." She faltered and began again, encouraged by the complete absorption in the blue eyes that watched her. "I want to make love with you, but I'm not very good at this."

The hard body she lay against went completely still, his hand closing almost painfully on her bottom. The blue gaze locked on hers registered shock, delight, and fierce pleasure.

"I want to make love with you, too, but, honey, you're dead wrong. You're *very* good at this."

He rolled sideways with her in his arms and surged to his feet.

"We're going to your bedroom," he said soothingly, reading the sudden apprehension in her darkened lavender eyes.

Lily sighed and buried her face against his neck.

# EIGHT

Moonlight spilled through the bedroom windows, throwing a pale path across the bed. Filtered through the feathery fronds of the hanging fern, the silvery light was laced with delicate leaves of shadow.

Trace slowly lowered Lily, the stroke of her body down the length of his as he set her on her feet sweet torture. Still holding her pressed against him, he yanked back the covers on the bed.

He captured her mouth with his. In some far corner of her mind, Lily felt the warm brush of his fingers against her midriff and heard the soft rasp of her zipper giving way, but his tongue was stroking the soft inner skin of her mouth and she couldn't concentrate on anything else.

Trace slid both palms inside the waistband of her loosened jeans and the fine wool thermal underwear she wore beneath them and pushed them both downward. Reluctantly, he lifted his mouth from hers.

"Sit down, honey," he murmured, and when she lifted heavy lashes to stare at him, uncomprehendingly, he felt a fierce surge of pleasure that she clearly was as trapped by desire as he. He pressed his open mouth to hers in a brief, hot kiss and gently pushed her to a sitting position on the edge of the bed before he knelt in front of her and bent to unlace her boots.

Lily smoothed her hands over the tousled thickness of his tawny hair, loving the silky slide of it through her fingers, before letting her hands explore further, tracing the curve of his ears and the soft skin beneath.

Trace tugged off her boots and dispensed with her jeans just as quickly. She sat on the edge of the bed dressed only in brief lavender lace panties, her hands cradling his face. Trace shrugged his unbuttoned shirt off his shoulders before he slid his arms around her waist and she tugged him closer, wrapping her arms around his neck. Wedged between her legs, her bare torso pressed against his, those velvety nipples crushed against his chest, while her mouth ardently returned the hot pressure of his, Trace wanted nothing more than to tip her onto her back against the sheets and take her with all the searing, driving need that shuddered through him. But some small, still sane, part of his brain reminded him that he had to go slow, so he forced himself to peel his protesting arms and body away from her and stand.

Hands shaking, he ripped the button open on his jeans and slid the zipper down.

"Wait!" Lily said softly, and stood on trembling legs, her hands covering his just inside the waistband of his jeans.

*Oh, God, no!* he thought with agony. *Please don't stop now!*

"Let me do it," she breathed, violet eyes lambent.

Relief nearly brought him to his knees.

"You want to?" he managed to get out.

"Yes," she whispered emphatically. "I want to. I don't

want you to just make love to me, I want to make love to you, too."

He bent and caught her mouth in a quick, deep kiss, his tongue surging into her mouth.

"Good," he rasped. "I want your hands on me."

Lily shuddered, her hands tightening with erotic reaction.

His hands slid out from under hers, fastening in her hair. Lily pushed the loosened jeans down over his hips, leaving him clad in white briefs.

"Sit down," she said.

He obeyed her gentle urging, releasing her hair when she bent to pull off his boots. His jeans quickly followed and, for a brief moment, she remained kneeling at his feet, her hands resting on his bare, hair-roughened thighs. The moonlight fell over her, throwing mysterious, lacy shadows over her upturned face and the velvety skin of her shoulders and the upward swell of her breasts. She was so beautiful, she took his breath, and Trace could wait no longer. He lifted her, pulling her on top of him as he fell backward on the bed, his hands sliding into the thick fall of her hair to cradle her head and hold her mouth to his.

He cupped her buttocks and moved her against him. Her small gasp against his mouth told him what he needed to know and he rolled sideways, his fingers brushing the smooth skin of her inner thigh, marveling at the velvety softness before he slid his fingers beneath the elastic to stroke her. Lily stiffened, the muscles of her thighs clenching in quick reaction.

"It's all right, baby," Trace murmured against her mouth. "I won't hurt you, I promise."

The quick panic in the lavender eyes so close to his faded to apprehension and, as his hand continued to stroke slowly, with gentle caresses that brought only surges of fiery pleasure and no pain, her lashes slowly drifted closed, her lips seeking his.

Trace groaned, his mouth widening over hers, his tongue entering her mouth with slow, steady thrusts that matched the movements of his hand between her legs. His fingers stopped and Lily murmured in protest at the loss of his touch as he stripped away the brief scrap of lavender lace. But then he settled his weight between her thighs and he was sleeker, better—so much better—and she groaned, her hips moving with helpless seeking.

"God, baby, you're so hot," he rasped. Driven by a need that was far past reason, he moved against her eager body, his passage eased by her own body's frantic need. "And so damn tight," he breathed. Pleasure surged over him as he slowly completed their union, his body fitting against hers as if it had finally found its other half and made him whole.

Lily was so caught up in her own body's demands that she felt no fear when Trace moved over her, blanketing her with his heavy weight. She knew only increased pleasure that it made his thrusts harder, deeper, and she responded with an instinctive sensuality that took his breath. She strained against him, holding him closer as something inside her coiled tighter until she felt as if she would fly apart.

"Trace," she cried in a soft, scared whisper.

"Let go, honey," he murmured against her breast. "I'm here."

And she did. The world exploded in rockets and fireworks while she clung to Trace's hard body. She'd barely recovered before Trace's world exploded, too, and he surged against her, his body jerking as he rode the same rockets that had earlier carried her.

His weight settled against her and Lily held him tightly, his breath rasping against the hollow between her shoulder and neck. He shifted to move off her and her arms tightened, pinning him against her.

"Don't go," she murmured, reluctant to end the joining of his body with hers, still stunned with the force of the pleasure she'd found.

He lifted himself up on his forearms, levering most of his weight from her and looked down into her face.

"I'm not going anywhere," he said softly, sifting his fingers through the tangle of her hair to smooth it against the snowy white pillow. "But I'm too heavy for you."

"No, you're not," she protested. Her hands slipped lower to press his hips against hers and his eyes darkened. "I don't want this to end."

Blue fire leapt in his eyes and he bent his head and brushed her mouth with his.

"This is never going to end," he said huskily, lifting his tawny head to look down at her with fiercely intent eyes. "Never." He shifted sideways, moving off her before pillowing her head against his shoulder, and bent to feather soft kisses over her closed eyes. His palm smoothed down the line of her body, tracing the inward curve of waist and the outward sweep of hip all the way to her knees before changing directions to move upward along the soft skin of her inner thigh. His hand lingered to brush over the soft triangle of black silk before continuing onward over the soft skin of her stomach. His forefinger tested the tiny hollow of her navel and her muscles jumped under his palm, her fingers tightening in reaction where they lay against his waist, and a smile curved her mouth under his.

"Ticklish?" he murmured, watching her lashes lift over surprised violet eyes.

"Yes," she whispered back. "I guess I am."

"You guess?" he echoed teasingly. "You mean this is the first time anyone ever tickled your belly button?"

"Yes," she said, her voice solemn, the smile fading from her lips.

Trace's heart clenched with protective fierceness. Whoever the man had been who made her fear sex, he'd taught her nothing about intimacy. Trace was both angered and glad, angered that someone had hurt her and glad that she would discover the small, intimate pleasures of sharing her body with him and not someone else.

His finger slowly brushed her navel, a smile growing as he felt her muscles jump again.

"Are *you* ticklish?" Lily asked, her fingers leaving his waist to trail in retaliation across his flat stomach, sensitive fingertips brushing the narrow strip of tawny hair that circled his navel.

"Nope," he said, his eyes half closing against the pleasure of her fingers moving against his skin. "Not there."

"Where?" she whispered against his mouth. "Here?" Her hand shifted lower and he caught his breath.

"No," he managed to get out. "Not there."

"Hm." Lily was having trouble breathing. "Where?"

Trace's hand caught hers and showed her where, wrapping her hand around that part of him that ached for her touch. His big body shuddered with the pleasure of her soft hand stroking him and his mouth closed hotly over hers, their bodies moving together with a growing heat that threatened to incinerate them.

Long moments later, Lily lay sprawled across his chest, both of them too exhausted to move.

Trace smoothed his palm up and down the soft line of her spine and pressed a kiss against the cloud of black hair beneath his chin.

"I've been looking for you all my life," he said huskily. "I don't ever want this to end. No more Saturday night good nights. I want a Sunday kind of love. I want the right to go to bed with you on Saturday night and kiss you awake and make love to you all over again on Sunday morning. I want to read the Sunday newspaper before we go to church, and eat dinner at my mom and dad's before we come back here and spend all afternoon making love all over again. All afternoon,'' he said, nuzzling her neck before muttering, ''What the hell, I may keep you in bed all week.''

Lily stiffened, and she tilted back her head to search his face. Surely he couldn't mean . . . ?

''I love you,'' he said softly, blue eyes tender as they stroked over her upturned face. ''And I want to marry you and spend every Sunday with you, and have babies, and cherish you all my life until we're both old and gray.''

''Oh, Trace,'' Lily's voice was wobbly, and tears welled before spilling over to make silvery tracks down her cheeks. She buried her face against his neck, her arms tightening fiercely around his muscle-layered ribs.

''Hey,'' he said. ''You're not supposed to cry, you're supposed to be happy.''

Lily only cried harder, and by the time he'd petted and soothed and kissed her, tears and kisses had turned to fast breathing and pounding pulses and, once again, they made love. Long slow love that was tender and fierce and held promises, and left them sated, drifting into sleep in each other's arms.

The warm pillow that cushioned Lily moved, shifting her, and she protested drowsily, arms tightening. Warm, enfolding arms hugged her against the warm muscles she lay against and lips brushed kisses against her cheek and temple.

''I have to go, honey,'' Trace whispered against her neck. ''It's nearly three A.M. and Mrs. Carson's going to be gossiping about us tomorrow as it is.''

"No," she mumbled in protest, arms clinging to him.

Trace felt a surge of pleasure that she didn't want him to leave. He'd lain awake for hours holding her, wondering why she hadn't told him that she loved him. *She does*, he thought. *And she would have said the words if I hadn't worn her out making love to her. I'll tell her again when she's awake, really awake.* But for now, she was barely conscious. He smoothed the tumble of black silk back off her forehead and smiled tenderly down at her barely open eyes. He kissed her again and gently pulled away from her. Though she protested sleepily, she curled up beneath the comforter, snuggling into the warmth left by his body.

He dressed quietly, returning to stand by the bed and look down at the woman curled in the bed, hugging his pillow. A flood of tender possessiveness shook him and he bent over her, kissing her sleeping face one last time before reluctantly leaving.

Lily woke at dawn, and for a few blissful, unaware moments, she felt the slight soreness and twinges from muscles long unused and remembered only the incredible heights of pleasure Trace had taken her to the night before. But the smile faded from her face as she remembered the words he spoke and her heart twisted with agony.

*He loves me, he wants to marry me!* What irony! For weeks now, Lily had known that what she felt for Trace far exceeded lust for his undoubtedly sexy body. She loved him, too, but she'd never thought for a moment that Trace could be feeling the same. The belief that he wanted only an affair had freed her to indulge her compulsive need to spend time with him and share passionate kisses that had led to their making love. She'd always assumed that sooner or later the affair would end, but had been equally sure that it would be Trace who would end it when he grew tired of her and moved on to another pretty face.

The fact that *she* would end it, and far sooner than she could bear to think about, was almost more than she could bear. But she had to tell Trace the truth, and the sooner the better.

Trace knocked on Lily's door several hours later. He had an uneasy feeling in his gut. There'd been something in her voice when she'd called him earlier that set alarm bells jangling. He knocked again and waited, hands propped on hips, eyes narrowed thoughtfully as he stared at the door.

Lily pulled open the door, her heart diving as her gaze inventoried the familiar, beloved lines of Trace's face. He was wearing the ever-faithful faded Levis that fit like a second skin, black boots, and the bomber jacket that always reminded her of that earthshaking kiss under the street lamp. Beneath the brown leather, a black pullover sweater covered his broad chest.

"Come in," she said, and held the door wide for him to enter. When he would have pulled her into his arms, she pretended not to notice and concentrated on carefully closing the heavy wooden door.

Trace saw the way she paused, and he didn't miss the slight squaring of her shoulders before she turned back to him. There was an air of fragility about her that worried him, her eyes bright jewels against the delicate pale oval of her face. The blue wool dress she wore was buttoned to her throat, the long sleeves covering her arms to her wrists, the skirt falling to midcalf. It was as though she'd purposely armored herself against him.

"What's wrong, honey?" he asked, and the feeling of dread grew stronger when his soft question resulted in her slender fingers twisting even more tightly the already damp handkerchief she held.

"I have to talk to you, Trace," she said, her voice almost desperate.

"All right," he answered, and followed her when she walked into the living room. She paused, her hands braced on the back of an upholstered armchair. "What is it?" he prompted, worried as her pale face seemed to grow even more coolly remote. "We can fix whatever's wrong honey."

Her face twisted, losing its reserve to reveal a depth of vulnerable hopelessness that tore at his heart.

"No," she choked out. "Not this. We can't fix this."

Trace wanted to pull her into his arms, but she looked so fragile that he was afraid she'd break if he touched her, so he forced himself to stay where he was.

"We can," he said with quiet conviction. "Just tell me, honey."

"You'll hate me," she whispered, pain glazing lavender eyes in their thicket of black lashes.

"No." He rejected the very thought. "Nothing you could tell me would ever make me hate you."

"I can't marry you, Trace," she said, her hands clenching into fists against the green upholstery.

"Is that all?" Relieved, Trace's muscles relaxed. He'd expected her to have second thoughts about commitment. "I know it's going to take you a while to get used to the idea, Lily, but—"

"No," she interrupted him, shaking her head in rejection. "You don't understand. I can never marry you Trace."

"Why not?" he asked, expecting to hear a list of uncertainties. He wished she were more sure of him and of his love, but he was confident that he could convince her in time.

Lily bit her lip, nibbling until she tasted the brassy flavor of blood, while she stared at him. She didn't want to tell him, she thought with desperate intensity. Dear God, how she didn't want to tell him.

But she had no choice. She should have told him long before.

"Because I'm already married," she whispered.

He stared at her, unblinking. He'd heard the words, he understood the words, his mind just refused to believe them.

"You're already married?" he said slowly, as if repeating the words would make them more believable.

"Yes."

"You're already married," he repeated, the words slowly sinking in. "I don't believe this," he said softly, almost to himself, but Lily heard him clearly. "If you're married, where's your husband?" he asked, staring at her with a slowly easing numbed disbelief.

"I don't know," she said through throat muscles stiff with emotion.

"You don't know," he repeated, his disbelief slowly replaced by a confused anger that was growing by leaps and bounds. "When did you see him last?"

"Five years ago," she answered.

"Five years . . ." he repeated, relief surging through him. "That's not being married, that's a separation, a long separation. So divorce him."

"I can't," she said softly, tensing and holding her breath while she waited for him to explode.

Trace's body went ominously still, thick lashes narrowing over sapphire-blue eyes while he stared at her consideringly.

"Why not?" he demanded softly, trying to hold on to his temper.

Lily had known he would ask. She'd also known that she couldn't answer. Not only could she simply not bring herself to reveal the ugly truth behind the short-lived marriage, but she couldn't expose Trace to the danger of befriending her. Derek had not only threatened her, but anyone who helped her. In the five years since she'd disappeared from Los Angeles and their travesty of a marriage, she'd never once contacted the few friends who might have helped her, no matter how desperate she had become.

"I just can't," she said simply, knowing she could never risk filing for divorce. Of necessity, her attorney would have to notify Derek. He would know where she was, and she knew he would come looking for her, and when he found her, he would find out about Trace. Neither of them would be safe. She couldn't risk that.

"That's not an answer," he ground out. "Why can't you? Do you still love him?"

"No!" Lily rejected the thought with revulsion. "I just can't divorce him, I can't tell you any more than that."

"I can't accept that," Trace argued with heat. "I love you, and whether you'll admit it or not, I believe you love me. I want to marry you, and we can't until you divorce your husband."

Lily felt a thousand wounds, all bleeding her life away, and steeled herself to say the words that would send him out of her life forever.

"I never said I loved you," she said with as much calm as she could muster. "And I never said I wanted to marry you."

Trace felt her words hit him like bullets from a .350 magnum, and he reeled under the impact.

"Are you telling me that all you wanted was a one-night stand?" he demanded thickly, disbelievingly.

"I didn't say that . . ." She couldn't bring herself to actually lie to him. "But I thought that's all you wanted from me."

"You were wrong," he ground out, his blue eyes fiery.

"I'm sorry," she whispered helplessly, her eyes filling with hot tears that burned.

"Lily . . ." Torn apart by her tears, Trace took a step toward her but was stopped by her immediate withdrawal.

"I think it would be best if you leave now," she managed to get out, her voice wobbling and thick with tears. "And that we not see each other again."

Frustrated, knowing in his gut that she wasn't telling him the truth, Trace stood stock-still, watching her for a long moment before he nodded.

"All right, if that's the way you want it, that's the way we'll leave it—for now," he said. "But this isn't over, Lily. Sooner or later you're going to tell me whatever it is that you're so afraid of, and while you're thinking about it . . ." He paused, forcing himself not to reach out for her. "Think about this: you're mine. You gave yourself to me last night and whatever hold that son of a bitch still has over you, he's not getting you back!"

With one last, sweeping glance, Trace spun on his heel and left, the storm door slamming on his back. Lily stood unmoving, leaning for support against the high-backed chair until the noise of the Camaro's engine had died away from the street in front of the house.

*I did the right thing,* she told herself. But her heart didn't listen and she crumpled from the pain, stumbling to the sofa to curl up on its long length and giving in to the sobs that wrenched her slim frame.

"She's married?" Jesse's voice was incredulous. "You're kidding!"

"No, damn it, I'm not kidding," Trace growled, barely missing his thumb as he pounded a nail into the oak replacement for the worn stair tread. "She's married."

"I'll be damned," Jesse whistled, long and low. "I'm sure Sarah didn't know or she would have said something."

"I doubt that anyone knows. I could tell Lily would rather have cut out her tongue than tell me." Trace wiped his forearm across his forehead, leaving a trace of sawdust against his skin, and reached for another nail. "That was right before she told me she thought we shouldn't see each other anymore."

"Hmm," Jesse said, and made another swipe across the banister with the sandpaper. "So where's her husband?"

"She doesn't know." Trace let off some of his frustration by pounding the hammer against the innocent nail with enough force to send it slicing through the oak like a hot knife through butter. One blow leveled it with the hard wood. "She hasn't seen him in five years."

Jesse grunted noncommittally and squinted an eye at the banister he was polishing.

"So why doesn't she divorce him? Five years is a hell of a long time." He fingered a still-rough spot on the glossy wood and smoothed the fine-grained paper across it once again.

"That's what I said," Trace answered, and sat back on his heels. "She said she can't."

"Can't?" Jesse shot him a disbelieving glance. "What does that mean, can't? Anybody can get a divorce these days, it's not all that hard."

"Yeah, well, that's what I thought. But she said she can't. Period. No explanation."

"Well," Jesse said consideringly. "It doesn't seem likely that she still cares about the guy after five years. Why do you think she can't?"

"I don't know." Trace frowned. He didn't want to believe that she still cared about her husband. *Ex-husband*, he told himself grimly. He refused to call him Lily's husband, whoever he was. "I do know that she's afraid of men. She avoids them like the plague. I always assumed it was because somebody gave her a bad time, maybe even raped her, but I don't know now. Maybe it was her husband. What do you think?''

''I think maybe you're on to something; if it was her husband, that's a pretty damn good reason for a woman not to see him for five years. And maybe that's why she won't divorce him, because if she filed a case, she'd have to see him in court. But if she won't talk about it, how are you going to find out?''

''Sarah told me that up until five or six years ago, every move Lily made was reported in the press,'' Trace said slowly, lashes narrowing thoughtfully over sapphire eyes. ''It makes sense that they would have covered her wedding, doesn't it?''

''Makes sense to me, Sherlock. Now what?''

''Now I call Mark Daly and have him run a check on her, and hope he turns up a name for a husband.''

''Then what?''

''Hell, I don't know.'' Trace thrust impatient fingers through his hair. ''But at least I'll know what I'm up against. Maybe I'll get some idea about why she says she can't divorce him.''

Jesse eyed his friend. He'd known Trace since grade school and he'd never seen him in this kind of a state before. He'd watched Trace's single-minded pursuit of Lily with amusement, for it reminded him vividly of his own head-over-heels love for Sarah. There wasn't a doubt in his mind that Lily was Trace's forever-after love, just as Sarah was his. He tried to imagine what he would have done if Sarah had been married to someone else. It didn't bear thinking about.

Trace glanced up and found Jesse looking at him with sympathy. He forced a grin.

''I'll bet you're sick of hearing about my problems,'' he said. ''Especially with your own wedding only a few weeks away. I didn't mean to rain on your parade.''

"Don't be an idiot," Jesse said with easy affection. "Just because I'm so happy I'm walking around babbling doesn't mean I'm completely incompetent."

"Come to think of it," Trace grinned, "you are a real pain in the butt." He glanced down at the repaired stair tread before his gaze roamed inspectingly over the entryway. Sawdust spattered across the waxed oak flooring. "Leave it to you and Sarah to pick an old Victorian to buy. Couldn't you have picked something a little newer? Like maybe a house that was only fifty years old? Then maybe we wouldn't have worn a new set of calluses getting this place ready for you two to move into!"

"We like old houses," Jesse argued without heat. "Newer houses just don't have the same character. Besides, the big rooms are great for a family. There are five bedrooms in this one."

"Terrific!" Trace eyed him wryly. "Have you told Sarah that you plan to fill up all five of those bedrooms?"

"Sure." Jesse's grin held a wealth of male complacency.

"And she agreed?"

"Of course. She agrees with everything I say."

"Hah!" Trace roared with laughter. "You're lying through your teeth, James! And if she's got you conned into believing that, she's going to lead you a merrier dance than I thought!"

The two continued the repairs to the stairway, Jesse's companionship relieving some of the lonely ache that filled Trace's heart. He missed Lily so damn much he could hardly stand it, and it had only been three days since she told him she didn't want to see him again. Three long, lonely, endless days and even longer nights.

It took Mark Daly less than forty-eight hours to collect a folder of information an inch thick on Lily Townsend and the man she married.

"Is this all you've got on him?" Trace demanded, scanning the sheaf of papers in his hand.

"Isn't that enough?" Mark snorted, leaning back in his chair and propping his crossed ankles against the open bottom drawer of the metal desk. The small, square office with its single window had stacks of files piled on top of every available flat surface. The CastleRock City Police Department was short on staff and long on workload. "There's enough there to convince me that the guy's a slug. You want more?"

"No," Trace answered absentmindedly, reading the copy beneath the newspaper photo of a much younger, more innocent-appearing Lily, her arm held by a tall, black-haired man with a deep tan and smooth, practiced smile. Derek Kenyon. Even the name made him see red. "What the hell did she see in him?"

"Well, he's good-looking enough, I guess," Mark answered. "And if you look at his track record, Lily's not the only one who fell for his line. He's been married half a dozen times, always to rich women. In the last five years, he's been linked with several more women, most of them either very young or a lot older than he is. If I had to guess, I'd say that's how he makes his living—conning women."

Trace gave a disgusted growl and tossed the sheaf of papers down atop Mark's already nearly buried desk.

"But you didn't turn up a thing on Lily in the last five years? How could someone as beautiful, young, and successful as Lily just disappear? She married Kenyon and the papers were full of it, then six months later she's gone. No one knows where. There are a few speculative articles in the gossip columns and then nothing. Zip. Zero. Total silence. This just doesn't make sense, Mark."

"Well, in the first place," Mark commented, eyes narrowing in thought, "she was less a performer and more a songwriter in the years after she became a teenager and before she married Kenyon.''

''So? What difference does that make?''

''The performer in the spotlight gets the publicity, and everybody knows the title of the number-one song, but how familiar is the face of the person who wrote the song?''

Trace looked thoughtful as he mulled over the logic of Mark's words.

''Sometimes you know the name of the composer, especially if he performs his own songs. Like Kris Kristofferson, for instance. Did you know that he wrote 'Me And Bobby Magee' before he recorded it himself? I sure didn't. If I'd been asked, I would have guessed that Janis Joplin wrote it.''

''Yeah,'' Trace answered slowly. ''You're right. But what does that have to do with Lily?''

''It was easier for her to drop out of sight, even though she was famous, because she hadn't been as high profile,'' Mark explained patiently.

''It's still hard for me to believe that she could just disappear without a trace.''

''Hah,'' Mark snorted. ''It's easier than you think. Just ask the numbers of divorced wives hunting ex-husbands for delinquent child support! If you *really* want to drop out of sight, it's more than possible. Especially if you're willing to sever all contact with former acquaintances, change your lifestyle, and switch careers completely.''

''Damn,'' Trace muttered, the reality of what Lily's life had been like sweeping over him. Where had she spent those missing five years, and with whom? ''She gave up everything that was familiar to her. That takes a hell of a lot of incentive.''

''Mmhh,'' Mark mused. ''Makes you wonder what he did to her, doesn't it?''

Trace's hand closed into a fist on top of the stack of papers. The possibilities were endless, and even contemplating the simplest of them was enough to set his teeth on edge and rouse a lust for killing that fogged his vision with a red haze.

''Yeah,'' he growled. ''I think I can guess. What I don't understand is, why won't she divorce him?''

''Hard to say.'' Mark eyed his friend over the edge of his ever-present coffee mug. ''Women are funny. Maybe she still loves him.''

Trace growled a curse, but didn't refute Mark's logic. *Maybe she does still love him,* he reflected bleakly. The thought made him ill.

# NINE

Two weeks without Trace was hell. Lily's life was lonely and empty without him. She hadn't realized just how much his presence had been woven into the daily fabric of her life until he was no longer there. He'd colored her days and filled them with companionship, an unfulfilled desire that still simmered through her veins, and a warm sense of being loved and needed.

*I don't want to do this,* Lily thought, staring at the brick walls of Grace Lutheran Church. She dreaded facing Trace, but at the same time, her heart was beating faster with anticipation. It was six twenty-five in the evening and the wedding rehearsal was scheduled to begin promptly at six-thirty. Her fingers closed tightly over the steering wheel. Would he talk to her, or would he refuse to speak? Either option was unpalatable to Lily.

She forced her gloved fingers to loose their grip on the steering wheel and got out of the car, her heels crunching on the surface of the snowy parking lot. The collar of her calf-length wool coat was turned high around her neck and she held it closer against the penetrating cold, her long hair almost invisible against the black wool, and hurried across the frosty parking lot and up the steps to the church.

Light, warmth, and laughter greeted her when she pulled open the heavy wooden door and stepped into the vestibule.

"Lily!" Jeannie McFadden bustled out of the small anteroom and smiled with relief. "We were beginning to worry about you."

She caught Lily's arm and hurried her into the little room, already crowded with Sarah and her attendants, including the little four-year-old flower girl and her mother.

"There you are," Sarah called, pushing through the crowd of laughing, chatting women to reach them. "I was beginning to think we were going to have to send out a search party! Is everything all right?"

"Fine," Lily managed a smile. "Just fine."

"Great." Sarah was too distracted by the hubbub around her to notice that the smile didn't reach Lily's eyes. "Oops, it's time."

Jeannie clapped her hands for attention.

"All right, everybody, let's get lined up!"

The little flower girl moved with solemn importance to stand before Jeannie and the other women moved into position. While Jeannie was rearranging the sequence of two of the bridesmaids, Lily quickly shrugged out of her coat and dropped it over a metal folding chair in one corner.

"You're next in line, Lily."

Lily obeyed Jeannie's beckoning finger and dutifully took her place, while Sarah's mother consulted her typewritten list.

"You're paired with Mark Daly, Lily."

Lily nodded in acknowledgment, glad that Jeannie didn't require a response, because she didn't think she could have answered coherently. Butterflies were dancing nervously in her stomach and she pressed a calming hand against her midriff, drawing in a deep breath to settle the fluttering. The sound of organ music swelled, penetrating the little room, and Jeannie clapped her hands for attention.

"Now remember, ladies, move in time to the music, and wait until the attendant in front of you reaches the fourth pew from the door before you start." She opened the door to the vestibule, propping it open with the floor lock, and smiled down at the little flower girl. "You're first, Stacey. You're not nervous, are you?" The little girl shook her head and Jeannie gave her an encouraging hug. "Good. There's nothing to worry about. Just remember to take slow steps in time with the music and pretend to toss flower petals from your basket onto the carpet. Here we go."

Lily watched Jeannie lead the little girl from the room and felt a moment of sheer panic. But the line of attendants was already moving and it was too late to escape. She smoothed damp palms down the lilac wool covering her hips and stepped forward, carefully blanking all expression from her face.

Trace stood at the altar next to Jesse and watched the entrance intently. For the tenth time in as many minutes, he shot an impatient look at his wristwatch.

"What's taking them so long?" he muttered impatiently.

"They'll be here," Jesse said calmly. "Do you have any idea how many women there are in that little room?"

"I don't care how many women are in there," Trace growled. "I only care about one of them."

"You're sure she'll show up?" Jesse asked.

"I'm sure," Trace answered, never taking his gaze from the doorway. "Lily would never let Sarah down, no matter how she feels about seeing me again. She knows how important this wedding is to my sister."

"I still don't see how you're going to manage to spend any time with her. Sarah and your mom told me that the bridesmaids are paired with the groomsmen for the whole night. That means dinner and dancing, too, so how are you going to get her alone?"

"I've already taken care of that. Josh is going to take over my partner after dinner, and Mark is taking his."

"Oh, yeah?" Jesse cocked an eyebrow at Trace. "How much did that cost you?"

"Nothing." Trace shot a sideways glance at Jesse's skeptical face, and the stern lines of his face broke into a grin. "Not after Josh got a good look at Angela last night when she came by the house. And Mark owes me a favor."

"Ahh." Jesse grinned knowingly. "Leave it to Josh."

"Yeah, my little brother ought to be the one with the reputation. Why is it that I get teased about blondes all the time and he manages to keep such a low profile?"

Jesse shrugged. "Probably because he tends to love 'em and leave 'em, literally. He's only around for a few weeks and then he takes off again for parts unknown."

"Yeah." Trace grinned as the subject of their conversation strolled down the side aisle toward them. "Speak of the devil. Here comes the travelin' man himself."

"Stop calling me that," Josh growled without heat. "When is this thing going to get started? At this rate, it'll be time for the wedding and we still won't be done with rehearsal."

"Mom's probably trying to stretch this out as long as possible to keep you at home," Trace commented. "Have you gotten the 'why don't you stay in Iowa and get married' lecture yet?"

"Yeah, at least twice." Josh heaved a long-suffering

sigh. "I told her I was already married in a secret ceremony and had a wife and twelve kids in Mexico."

"Really?" Jesse eyed him. "Did it work?"

"Nope."

Trace listened to the two exchange small talk while they waited and his attention drifted.

*Two weeks. Two weeks is too damn long,* he thought bleakly. Why had he agreed not to see Lily? He should never have accepted her decision not to see him again; he should have refused to let her cut him out of her life. Only the knowledge that Sarah's wedding would bring her back within speaking distance, touching distance, had kept him from knocking on her door.

The organ player switched to the wedding march and Trace straightened, muscles going taut. The flower girl stepped through the doorway and moved down the red-carpeted aisle, followed by two of Sarah's college roommates. The groomsmen stood to the left of the doorway and moved forward as the bridesmaids came through, taking their arm to escort them to the altar.

Lily appeared in the doorway and Trace caught his breath. She was wearing a dress that was a simple, straight sheath of lavender wool that ended above her knees, the simple lines faithfully following the curves of her body. Matching lavender pumps covered her feet below slim ankles and curvy, silk-clad legs. Her hair was loose; tucked behind her ear on one side, it cascaded over her other shoulder and spilled in a silky ebony fall over her breast.

Mark Daly was her escort, and as he stepped forward and she slid her hand through the crook of his arm, he bent forward and whispered to her. She smiled up at him and Trace knew a fierce desire to punch his longtime friend. They walked toward the altar in slow, measured steps. Trace watched them come with narrowed eyes, oblivious to anyone else in the room.

Lily saw Trace the moment she stepped into the doorway and her heart stopped beating before lurching into a ragged, heavy beat. His beloved face was completely expressionless, his blue gaze fastened on her with narrow-eyed intensity.

"Hi." Mark Daly took her arm and bent to smile at her. "I have to warn you, my sense of timing and rhythm is awful, so you're going to make sure we stay in step, right?"

"Right." Lily returned his friendly smile, grateful for his unknowing support.

They moved slowly down the aisle and Lily kept her gaze on the couple in front of them, carefully avoiding looking at Trace although she could feel his eyes on her. They reached the foot of the three shallow, carpeted steps leading to the altar and Mark released her arm. Lily let her glance rest on Trace for one brief moment before she and Mark separated to walk to opposite sides of the altar. That brief glance was enough to break her heart. His fathomless blue eyes watched her, his face expressionless as he nodded in brief acknowledgment. Lily returned his silent greeting with a slight inclination of her head, bleeding inside at the loss of the warm male approval and welcome she'd always seen on his handsome face. She swallowed the tears that clogged her throat and struggled for control.

The organ music stopped and Lily realized that while she'd been fighting her emotions, Sarah had walked down the aisle on Gavin's arm and was standing beside Jesse, fingers threaded through his while Pastor Larson walked them quickly through the details of the service.

". . . then you take the wedding ring from the best man," Pastor Larson instructed.

Jesse looked at Trace. The groomsman standing behind Trace nudged him.

"With luck, he'll stay awake and not forget to bring the ring," the man drawled with a grin.

"I won't forget," Trace assured Jesse, and threw a scowling glance over his shoulder. " 'Course, Josh might not show up for the wedding at all. He's forever taking off for unknown places at the drop of a hat."

Lily's gaze sharpened as she realized that the man standing behind and slightly to the left of Trace was Sarah's brother, Josh. Unlike Trace and Sarah, his thick hair was brown, with sun-bleached shadings, but his eyes were the same brilliant blue and the hard bones of his face had the same distinctive high cheekbones and determined jaw. He and Trace were nearly the same height, but Josh wasn't quite as brawny, although beneath the casual slacks and sweater he wore, his body held a leashed power that was easily discernible.

"Not this time—I couldn't miss my baby sister's wedding." He grinned at Sarah and the hearts of both Trace and Lily clenched at the look of deep contentment that passed between Jesse and his bride.

Her gaze moved compulsively back to Trace to find him watching her with an intensity that shaded immediately to impersonal reserve before he turned his attention to the pastor.

". . . and then you kiss the bride."

Jesse leered at Sarah and caught her in his arms, bending her over his arm until her long hair nearly brushed the crimson carpet. She laughed up at him before he kissed her quickly and lifted her upright.

"Like that?" he asked the pastor, while the other members of the wedding party laughed, whistled, and cheered.

"Well," the Pastor said wryly, eyeing the flushed, smiling bride-to-be. "I'm sure the audience will love the show, but I'm not sure Sarah's veil will make it through the ceremony."

"He's right," Sarah said, laughing at a nonrepentant Jesse. "I promise he'll behave, Pastor Larson."

"Good." The white-haired pastor smiled benignly at the young couple. He'd known both of them since they were toddlers just beginning Sunday school and he had no doubt that Sarah could make Jesse behave. "Then all we have left to run through is the exit. After you kiss her, Jesse, then you both turn to face the congregation, I introduce you as Mr. and Mrs. James, and you walk hand-in-hand to the vestibule. Each of the groomsmen and bridesmaids meet in front of the altar and fall in step behind you in pairs." He glanced around at the upturned faces. "Does everyone understand?" The nods of agreement drew an answering nod of satisfaction from him. "Good. Mrs. Anderson, the music, if you please."

The wedding march began, and Sarah and Jesse started down the carpeted aisle. Directly behind them, Trace moved forward and took the arm of Angela Parker, Sarah's college roommate and maid of honor.

Lily watched him smile at the pretty redhead and take her arm and felt a stab of jealousy so strong it nearly doubled her over.

*Dear God*, she thought. *How am I ever going to get through this?*

Blindly, she stepped forward when the line moved and took Mark's arm.

By the time the laughing group had run through the ceremony three times, Lily felt numb. Her face felt frozen in a permanent smile and she had no idea what she'd said in response to conversation. As they walked down the aisle for the last time and split up to collect their coats, she felt the beginning throb of a headache at her temples and fervently hoped that she'd be able to get through the next hour. She knew very well she wouldn't be able to choke down more than a few bites of the dinner and hoped fervently that Sarah wouldn't be offended when she left early.

"Can I give you a lift to the Lakeshore, Lily?" Mark asked beside her, taking her coat from her and holding it while she slipped her arms into the sleeves.

"Thank you, but no, Mark," she replied with a polite smile. "I have my car outside."

"All right, I'll see you at the restaurant, then. Sarah tells me we're paired for dinner."

Lily returned his grin and wave of good-bye and watched him thread his way through the crowded vestibule, stopping to speak with Trace.

*He's nice,* she thought. And better yet, his good manners provided a welcome cushion between her and Trace. She tugged on black leather gloves and followed Gavin and Jeannie McFadden out the church's front door and down the frosty steps.

Trace watched her interchange with Mark, his hands closing into fists when Mark held her coat and she smiled up at him.

"He's just being a gentleman."

Josh's voice penetrated his dark thoughts, but Trace didn't move his gaze from Lily's slim figure. He watched with relief when Lily shook her head and Mark walked away from her. The police lieutenant patiently made his way through the crowd until he reached Trace.

"I thought I better tell you I haven't forgotten she's your girl," Mark said, his brown gaze reading accurately the emotion simmering beneath Trace's hard features and remote blue eyes.

"I don't know if it matters, because she sure as hell doesn't act like *she's* remembering," Trace bit out, his gaze moving past Mark's shoulder to follow Lily's slim figure disappearing with his mother and father through the doorway.

"Oh, she remembers, all right," Mark said wryly. "When she took my arm to walk down the aisle, she was shaking. And every time she looked at you, I could feel her tense up. The lady isn't any happier about this than you are, Trace, I don't think she'd be here if she could possibly avoid it, and she damn sure wouldn't be with me."

Trace grunted noncommittally, only slightly mollified by the knowledge that Lily wasn't immune to the same pain that weighted his heart with lead.

"See you at the Lakeshore," Mark clapped a comforting hand against Trace's shoulder and left the church.

Trace watched him go with a thoughtful, narrow-eyed gaze, and it wasn't until the heavy, carved wooden doors shut Mark away from his view that he looked over his shoulder to find Josh leaning against the wall behind him, his arms crossed over his chest while he watched his older brother with curiosity.

"Pretty woman," Josh remarked, his keen gaze fastened on Trace's set features.

"Not pretty," Trace growled. "Beautiful. And she's taken, so keep your hands off."

"Hmm." Josh lifted an eyebrow and grinned lazily. "Don't tell me she's yours? She isn't even blonde."

Trace muttered an unprintable word at his brother and grabbed his coat from a high-backed wooden chair.

"Trace . . ." Josh's voice held laughter and pretended outrage. "Not in church!"

"Oh shut up," Trace snarled, "or you'll be walking to the Lakeshore."

The Lakeshore Supper Club had outdone itself. The long table reserved for the wedding party was covered in white linen, silverware glittered, crystal sparkled, and the flower arrangements were brilliant splashes of red poinsettias and fragrant evergreens and holly against the white tablecloths.

Lily sat between Mark Daly and a groomsman named Steve. To her relief, Trace sat across the table and down several chairs. Unfortunately, he was seated between Angela Parker and Beth Harris, both of whom clearly enjoyed his company.

*He doesn't seem to object to their company, either*, Lily thought with irritated jealousy as she cast a glance down the long table to find Trace laughing at something Beth had said. His eyes crinkled at the corners, his hard mouth curving in a way that brought a flood of memories of those same lips moving against hers.

*I refuse to sit here mooning over him,* Lily told herself with determination and forced her gaze away from the trio to concentrate on an anecdote Mark was telling about an escapade he and Jesse were involved in in high school.

". . . by the time Cole got there, Jesse, Trace, and I had already drag-raced five guys from Spencer and three from Estherville, not to mention the fastest cars from Spirit Lake. Cole was steaming that we'd taken his car without permission, but after he found out that we'd blown away every challenger, he was so proud of us that he forgot to be mad."

"Hah!" Steve snorted. "I remember hearing this story before and if I remember right, he got mad all over again when the cops arrested all of you and you had to call Gavin to come bail you out!"

"Well, yeah, he wasn't happy, that's for sure," Mark admitted, brown eyes gleaming with humor. "Come to think of it, neither was Gavin, and neither was my dad. But Cole was more mad at the cops than at us, although he threatened to skin us alive if we took his car again without asking. He also told us that if we wanted to race, he'd take us to the track.''

''And did you?'' Lily asked, drinking in the stories of Trace's teenage antics with helpless, thirsty fascination.

''Sure. We nagged him into taking us the next weekend. The rest of us drove practice laps, but Trace and Josh were the only ones with guts enough to drive in an actual race. Let me tell you,'' Mark assured her. ''Getting on a track with twenty other cars all driving hellbent for election is scary.''

''But Cole does it all the time,'' Lily commented.

''Sure, but that's Cole.'' The brief comment spoke volumes about the esteem Cole McFadden commanded. ''It's too bad he couldn't make it back for Sarah's wedding,'' Mark said. ''You'd like him, Lily.''

''What's he like?''

''Tall, broad—he's built like Trace and has the McFadden blue eyes and blond hair. Come to think of it, I'm glad he's not here,'' Mark cast a sideways, teasing glance at Lily. ''He's been around. Real smooth with women, that's Cole.''

''Hmm, sounds interesting,'' Lily teased back, thinking that she doubted it was possible for anyone to be more lethal with women than Trace. Dealing with one McFadden was enough for any female; she was just as glad Cole couldn't make the wedding.

She sipped her water, casting a sideways glance through her lashes down the table where Trace was charming his two dinner companions.

Trace glanced down the length of the long table just in time to see Lily burst into laughter at something Mark said. Her violet eyes lit with merriment, her soft mouth curving in a way that made his gut clench, remembering those same lips opening under his. His gaze grew hot as he watched Mark and Steve bend toward her, clearly enjoying her company. Steve picked up a crystal water pitcher and leaned closer while he refilled her water glass and Trace knew an overwhelming urge to surge out of his chair and punch the man he'd been friends with since grade school.

Neither Trace nor Lily could have told anyone what they had for dinner. Custom required that as best man, Trace must toast the happy couple, but after he sat down, he couldn't remember whether he'd drunk from his water glass or his champagne glass and he had no idea what he'd said.

At long last the dinner ended, and Sarah and Jesse led the exodus to the lounge next door, where a live band provided music for dancing.

Lily threaded her way through the group and caught Sarah's arm.

"Sarah," she said, smiling with affection when Sarah turned. Her friend's blue eyes sparkled with excitement, and she clung to Jesse's hand. "I had a lovely time, but I have to leave."

"Oh, no." Sarah's face fell and she looked at Lily, blue eyes darkening with concern. "What's wrong?"

"Nothing," Lily hastened to reassure her. "But I'm getting a headache and I—"

"You can't leave already," a deep voice interrupted. "You haven't danced with me yet."

Lily stiffened, violet eyes shading to deep lavender, and she turned slowly to face Trace.

"I don't think dancing is a good idea," she said. "I have a headache and I—"

"Dancing is the best thing for headaches," Trace said softly, and his hand captured hers, his calloused palm faintly rough against her soft skin. He tugged her one small step forward, and though she went hesitantly, at least she didn't refuse him. He heaved a silent sigh of relief and led her onto the small, polished dance floor. He didn't release her hand until he'd pulled it around his waist and then he let go so he could slide his arms around her and pull her close. He bent his head to rest his cheek against her temple, closing his eyes with an unvoiced groan as he drew in the fragrance of perfumed hair and skin.

Even though she knew that she wasn't being fair to Trace, Lily let him pull her close, the tight band of pain that had squeezed her heart ever tighter over the last few hours easing as she nuzzled her face against the soft wool of his blue sweater, inhaling the dearly familiar scent of aftershave and man that was uniquely his. She pressed against him, almost frantically registering the familiar fit of his hard planes against her soft curves.

"God, I've missed holding you," he ground out against her hair, his breath stirring the silky strands against his mouth.

Lily's arms contracted and she turned her face against his shoulder, tilting her head to look up at him through lowered lashes.

"I've missed you, too," she whispered, fighting the need to lift her mouth the few inches necessary to reach his.

"Have you?" he asked, his voice aching with the need to know she felt the same painful void of separation.

"Yes," she said, her voice trembling with the effort to suppress the emotion that threatened to overwhelm her. "Please," she managed to get out. "Don't do this to me, Trace. Let me go."

"Never," he said fiercely.

"You have to." Her voice broke, catching with the tears that roughened the already husky tones.

"No, I don't." Trace saw the tears that threatened to overcome her valiant effort to hold them back and bit back an oath. "Come on," he growled, reluctantly letting his arms release her and catching her hand in a grip that refused to be denied. "We're going someplace we can talk."

Lily let him collect their coats and say good night to Sarah and Jesse, dreading the tears that threatened to spill over, but just as determined not to let Trace override her own decision not to see him.

The Camaro was cold, and Lily huddled inside the warmth of her coat while Trace revved the big engine, waiting for it to warm up.

He looked sideways at Lily and found her profile etched by the dashlights against the dark night outside. His gaze stroked over the soft curve of brow and nose, the downward droop of her lips above the determined little chin, and a wave of tenderness washed over him. He smoothed his palm over the silky crown of her head and Lily turned her face to him, her violet eyes shadowed with pain and apprehension.

"Hey," he said softly, cupping her chin in his hand and smoothing his thumb along the soft fullness of her lower lip. "Stop worrying. We're going to be all right."

Before she could answer and deny his assertion, he bent toward her, pressing a warm, tasting kiss against her lips before turning back to the waiting car. Now warm, the engine growled throatily, the tires crunching against the snowy street as Trace eased away from the curb.

Silenced by the warm brush of his mouth against hers, Lily stared unseeingly out the windshield at the streetlights appearing and disappearing with patterned regularity outside the car.

*This is a mistake,* she thought. *I shouldn't be alone with him. All he has to do is touch me and my resolve weakens, and I can't let it. It isn't safe for him, and he'll only get hurt worse in the end.* She reflected bleakly that it seemed inconceivable that either of them could be hurt worse than they already were, but knew that it was true.

Trace slowed the car, pulling to a stop at the curb in front of her house and, still without speaking, opened Lily's door. They walked side-by-side up her walkway, their shoes crunching on the fresh skiff of snow that covered the shoveled concrete with a layer of cold white powder.

Lily fumbled in her little clutch purse for her keys, and didn't object when Trace took them from her fingers and moved to slide them into the metal lock. But the door moved inward without inserting the key, the latch clicking open. Trace frowned and glanced down at Lily, but she was staring at the door in surprise.

"Did you leave the door unlocked?" he asked.

"No, I never do," she answered, taking a sheltering step closer to him as he lifted a hand and pushed the door inward.

Only silence met them, and Trace stepped over the threshold, flicking the switch just inside the door to make the lamps spring into life. They lit the room with soft light and Trace and Lily stood just inside the door, their gazes moving across the comfortable room.

"You've had company," Trace commented as his keen gaze found a dirty plate and glass on the coffee table. The usually neat room had magazines shuffled across the top of the coffee table, a half full cup of coffee sitting atop a carelessly folded newspaper. "Were you expecting anyone?"

"No." Lily unconsciously tightened her grip on his hand and frowned at the clutter. "No, I can't imagine who . . ." Her gaze flicked around the room and zeroed in on the piano. The sheet music had been stacked haphazardly on the bench, and a single white sheet of paper was propped against the music rack.

An awful premonition of disaster seized her. She tugged her hand from Trace's, and with slow, halting steps, crossed the room to pick up the note.

"Oh, my God!"

The sheer panic in her voice had Trace striding across the room. He caught her shoulders and turned her to face him, cold fear freezing his heart as he saw her white face and the lavender eyes, blind with terror.

"Lily, what is it?"

# TEN

She didn't answer and Trace pried the crumpled paper from her stiff fingers. The words on the paper, bold black ink against the stark white, were simple: *I waited for you, but you haven't come home. I know you're as anxious to see me as I am to see you, my darling Lily. I'll be back. Your loving husband, Derek.*

Trace felt a rush of adrenaline, accompanied by exploding fury. At last, the bastard was within reach.

"Good," he said with fierce satisfaction. "Now I don't have to track him down."

"No," Lily whispered, the freezing, numbing fear that held her immobile easing its grip, allowing her to move. "No, you have to leave! Hurry, Trace, before he comes back!"

She tore her hand from his and raced across the room.

Trace followed her to her bedroom, halting abruptly in the doorway when he saw her throw open the closet doors and pull down a suitcase. She tossed it on the bed and flipped it open with a jerky movement before returning to the closet to snatch clothing, hangers and all, from the rod. She stuffed them in the case with no regard for wrinkles and disappeared inside the closet again to return with an armful of shoes.

Her movements were frantic, jerky. She looked up to see Trace standing in the doorway staring at her and burst into panicked speech.

"You have to leave! Now! Before he comes back! We have to get out of here!" Trace didn't move and she ran across the room, catching his forearm with cold fingers in a futile effort to turn him around, frantically pulling against his immovable bulk. "Please, Trace," she panted, almost in tears. "Please go!"

"Stop it, honey." Trace tried to control her, but she continued to tug on his arm, her frantic movements strengthened with fear. When she wouldn't be calmed, he wrapped his arms around her, pinning her arms against her sides, and caught her close against his hard body, continuing to murmur soothing nonsense and stroking her shivering body with slow, sure, comforting strokes.

"You don't understand," she said brokenly, her breath coming in great, shuddering sobs.

"I know I don't, sweetheart," he murmured, pressing kisses against her temple. "Tell me."

"He'll hurt you," she sobbed, her hands clenching into fists over the wool of his sweater. "He'll hurt you!"

"Like he hurt you?" Trace asked quietly, his body tensing as he waited for her answer.

"Yes," she got out between sobs. "Yes! Only worse. He'll kill you. He warned me that if I left him, he'd find me, and if anyone helped me, he'd kill them. He won't kill me, he'll just torment me and slap me until I beg him to stop the pain. But he'll kill you. He has a gun, Trace, you don't know him. Please, I couldn't bear it if he hurt you."

"He isn't going to hurt anyone, honey, least of all me.

And certainly not you. And you're not running away, either. You're going home with me. Any man who would beat a small, defenseless woman is a coward and not someone to be afraid of.'' He tipped her terrified, tear-drenched face back and looked into her eyes. ''You're not alone anymore, Lily. You don't have to be afraid of him. You have me and Josh and Jesse and Dad and Mark—and all the rest of CastleRock if you need it. He's never going to bother you again, not without going through me first.'' The stunned lavender gaze that met his reflected only shock and confusion. Trace decided she probably wasn't capable of understanding anything more, and with a last brief stroke of his palm down her slim back, he released her, tucking her safely against his side while he walked her out of the bedroom.

He picked up her purse when they passed through the living room.

''Wait,'' Lily protested as he snapped off the switch and threw the living room into darkness.

''What?'' he asked, stopping to look down into her worried face.

''I need my things.''

''What things?''

''My toothbrush, my nightgown . . .'' Her voice trailed off as he shook his head.

''You can borrow mine,'' he said impatiently, implacably. ''You're not staying here another minute. You're coming with me to my place. Where you belong,'' he added with grim finality, and walked her out of the house and tucked her into the Camaro.

He was silent on the drive to his house and Lily was equally quiet, occasional shudders still shaking her body with aftershocks. She hugged her coat around her, fighting the quivers that shook her with cold fear. Strangely enough, she realized, the mind-numbing terror that had gripped her when she recognized Derek's handwriting and read his signature was gone, banished by Trace's declaration that he wouldn't let Derek harm her. While her numbed brain was grappling with that distinctly amazing fact, Trace parked the Camaro in his garage and opened her door.

His hand under her arm was oddly impersonal, and when he bent his head to fit his key in the lock, the hard lines of his face were remote. He shoved the door open and looked down at her, his blue gaze almost clinical as he swept her pale face.

"Come on," he said. "You look like you're ready to collapse."

He led her into the house, locking the door behind them before he moved through the house, snapping on lights as they went. The house was a 1940's-era bungalow, with an air of solidity and permanence about it. The rooms reflected a bachelor's presence, without any of the knick-knacks, fluffed pillows, or green plants common to a woman's residence. But it was clean and neat, and blessedly warm to Lily's chilled body.

Lily climbed the stairs in front of Trace and hesitated as he moved past her to push open a door in the short hallway.

"This is the bathroom. There's an extra toothbrush in the cabinet, and I'll get you a shirt to sleep in." He stepped across the hall and pushed open another door into what was obviously a guest bedroom. "You can sleep in here. I'll find some extra blankets."

He turned and found her still standing in the same spot in the hallway, clutching her coat around her.

"Let me take your coat." He unbuttoned the black wool garment and slid it off, tossing it over his shoulder before his hands closed over her shoulders and he turned her, urging her gently into the bathroom. "Get in the shower," he instructed. "And stay in there long enough to get warm. You're so cold your teeth are chattering."

Lily knew her teeth weren't chattering, but she also knew she felt chilled through to her bones. She wasn't sure that it was the kind of cold that hot water would chase away, but it was worth a try. She unzipped her dress and stepped out of it, hanging it over a brass hook on the back of the door. With the same slow, careful movements, she removed her underclothes and folded them neatly before laying them across a white wicker hamper in the corner.

Shivering with a chill that radiated from the inside out, she adjusted the taps and stepped into the shower. The jets of warm water pulsed against her skin, slowly warming her, and she closed her eyes and tilted her face into the spray, letting it sluice over her. There was something lulling and soothing about the steady, rhythmic slide of warm liquid over her body and she stood motionless for long moments, face upturned, eyes closed, while the heated river flowed over her.

Trace rapped on the door panels and paused a moment to listen. The shower was still running, so he pushed open the door and stepped inside to drop a towel and one of his T-shirts on the cabinet.

"I put a towel and one of my shirts on the cabinet next to the sink, Lily," he called, narrowing his eyes against the steam that fogged the mirror and heated the room with humid warmth. "Are you all right?"

"I'm fine," Lily answered, her voice more alert. "And thank you."

"No problem." Trace registered the absence of panic from her voice and the return of her usual husky tones and knew a surge of heartfelt relief. "Stay in there until you're warm."

"I'll be out soon," she answered, disappointed when she heard the door click open and then close behind him.

Turning off the taps, she pulled her hair over her shoulder, water streaming from the thick rope as she twisted it. She pushed back the shower curtain and caught up the thick terry towel folded on top of the cabinet, rubbing and blotting the water from her hair and body before she tugged Trace's T-shirt over her head and wrapped the damp towel around her hair, turban-style, to keep the long, damp mane from soaking the shirt over her back.

The mirror was fogged with steam, and Lily wiped it clear with a hand towel, wincing at her reflection. Her face was pale, and the lavender eyes that gazed back at her were dark with apprehension.

*We're going to be all right,* she told herself reassuringly. *Derek can't find me here tonight, and tomorrow I'll leave town. Maybe I'll go south—Texas or Louisiana.* An instant twist of rejection moved through her. *I don't want to leave CastleRock. I don't want to leave my job, my students, my life here. And most of all,* she thought with painful, intense honesty, *most of all, I don't want to leave Trace.* The thought of never seeing him again was heart-rending, painful as the slash of a knife wound that left a gaping, bleeding hole where her heart had been.

*I'm sick of running. Will I never be safe?* she thought rebelliously, her thick lashes narrowing over darkened violet eyes. But she knew she couldn't risk staying, not when it was not only her life, but Trace's, that hung in the balance. Despite Trace's assurances, her fear of Derek's instability was still strong, fueled by memories of his past erratic behavior.

She pulled open the drawers in the cabinet, searching until she found a brush. Her hair was still damp when she pulled it free from the towel, and after combing out the tangles, she knew that she would have to brush it dry before falling asleep or it would be impossibly snarled in the morning. Brush in hand, with a sigh, she opened the door to the hall and stopped short in the doorway, eyes widening.

Trace leaned against the opposite wall, ankles crossed and arms folded across his chest, waiting for her, and when she opened the door, he stared at her for a long moment before pushing away from the wall. His shirt fell to midthigh on her, the round neckline threatening to slip off one shoulder. The material draped softly over the uptilted lift of her breasts and he knew without doubt that she was bare beneath the soft white knit. With iron control, he restrained the urge to reach out and crush her against him, and only the paleness of her face that made her thick-lashed lavender eyes appear even bigger and the vulnerable curve of her mouth kept him from doing just that. Besides, his love warred with the hurt he felt that Lily hadn't turned to him for protection. Although his intellect told him that her fear was too all-consuming to allow her to think rationally, still, his heart felt betrayed that she hadn't run to him for shelter.

*This is no time to ask her why she didn't trust you to keep her safe, McFadden,* Trace told himself. *She's emotionally exhausted, leave her alone.*

"Come on, honey," he said, and reached behind her to flip off the bathroom light. But when he did, his hand brushed against her wet hair. Frowning, he slid his fingers testingly into the thick mass at her nape. "Your hair's soaking wet. You can't go to bed like this, you'll catch pneumonia."

"I know," she answered huskily, barely controlling the need to lean forward and lay her aching head against his broad chest. "I'll brush it dry before I go to sleep."

"You're practically out on your feet as it is," he said, his blue gaze inspecting her wan face before he moved past her, his body brushing against hers as he stepped through the doorway into the bathroom. "Sarah left a hair dryer here the last time she house-sat for me."

He knelt and pulled open the cabinet door under the sink, rummaging in the depths until he found what he was looking for.

"Here it is." He stood with lithe ease, ignoring the flash of hot awareness as he turned back to Lily and found her watching him, the thick-lashed violet eyes dark with emotion. He changed his mind about sending her to the guest bedroom and instead, flicked off the light and put an arm around her shoulders. "First we'll dry your hair, then I'll tuck you in bed."

Lily went with him without protest. He was right; her arms felt leaden and the thought of the time and energy necessary to dry the long, thick mass of her hair by herself was daunting. Besides, being coddled by Trace held a sweetly irresistible attraction that she couldn't deny.

He led her into the bedroom at the end of the hall. The squat brass lamp on the oak nightstand next to the king-size bed was already lit, and it threw a pool of gold light across the blue down comforter that was folded halfway down the long bed, exposing plain white cotton sheets and pillowcases. Trace pulled the comforter further down the bed and bent to plug in the hair dryer behind the nightstand before he kicked off his shoes, pushed one of the pillows against the oak headboard, and sat down.

He pulled her down on the mattress in front of him and flicked on the hair dryer. For long moments, silence reigned, broken only by the hum of the dryer. Lily was half-asleep by the time her hair was dry.

"That should do it," Trace rasped, surprised that his voice would work. He stood, extricating himself with lithe ease. "Get under the covers," he ordered.

"I thought I was sleeping in the guest bedroom?"

Trace's jaw hardened, a muscle jumping tensely, and thick lashes narrowed over blue eyes that leapt with fire.

"Don't argue, Lily," he growled. "Just get in bed."

She considered arguing, but gave it up. She didn't want to sleep alone tonight. She slid between the sheets, her hair fanning against the pillowcase when she curled an arm under the soft cushion and turned on her side to watch him.

Outwardly, Trace ignored her, but he felt her gaze on his body like soft, stroking hands as he undressed. He stripped to his briefs, automatically hanging his clothes neatly away in the closet before crossing to the bed and sliding in beside her. He propped his back against the headboard, pulled the sheet and comforter up over his lap, and looked down at her. She was watching him, the pale skin of her face glowing with soft color across her cheeks. Trace forced himself to ignore the answering leap of heat in his own body.

"Why are you angry with me, Trace?" Lily asked softly.

"I'm not angry," he answered. "I'm disappointed."

"Disappointed?" She sat upright, crossing her legs Indian-style, and frowned at him in confusion.

"Yeah, disappointed. Why didn't you tell me why you were so afraid?"

"Oh, Trace . . ." Lily could feel the hurt beneath the level words, she could see it deep in his blue eyes. "I couldn't involve you in the mess I've made of my life, especially not when it could get you killed."

Trace growled an oath that told her clearly what he thought of that possibility.

"Let me tell you something, sweetheart, any man who gets his kicks out of terrorizing a woman is a bully and a coward, and the chances that he'll have the guts to face a man are mighty small." Trace's voice held bone-deep certainty. "Besides," he added grimly, "I'm looking forward to meeting him, and I hope to God he tries something."

"But, Trace . . ." Lily began, fear widening her eyes at the thought of Trace confronting Derek. "You don't understand. He's dangerous—I don't think he's mentally stable."

"Maybe he's not." Trace's eyes gleamed a deep sapphire beneath tawny brows. "But that still doesn't make him superman. And I think that's what he's become in your mind, Lily—superman, or his evil equivalent. He isn't supernaturally powerful, Lily; no mortal man is, and he's not dealing with a small, fragile woman this time. Do you really believe that if we fought, I'd lose?" There was an element of incredulous, insulted male pride underlying his deep tones.

Taken aback, Lily stared at him. Could he be right? Had fear inflated Derek's image in her mind until he'd assumed supernatural proportions? The longer she thought about it, staring unblinkingly at Trace with unseeing violet eyes whose gaze had turned inward, the more likely it seemed. Did she really think Trace couldn't protect her from Derek?

The unequivocal answer that came from deep within her was immediate and resolute, a resounding no!

Trace watched the lavender gaze refocus on him, lit with dawning certainty, while the fear faded from the violet depths and the tension eased and faded from her slim body.

"No," she said softly, amazed discovery vying with deep conviction in her husky tones. "No, I don't believe he'd have a chance."

"Good." That brief word hardly conveyed the fierce surge of exultant pride that lifted Trace's broad, bare chest as he exhaled. "Then you'll stop worrying about your ex-husband."

"He isn't my ex-husband," Lily said in a small, guilty voice.

"He will be," Trace said with conviction, the hard lines of his face set with determination. He caught the brief flicker of uncertainty that moved across her features and tensed. "Do you have a problem with that?" he asked softly, his voice holding dangerous dark shades.

"I should have told you." Lily looked him straight in the eye, wincing at the storm of emotion that roiled there. She drew a deep breath; confessing was difficult, even with Trace. "I'd like to be able to tell you that if I'd known I was more than just another affair to you, I would have told you about Derek, but I'm not sure I would have, even then."

"Why not?" he demanded gently.

"Because . . ." She drew a deep breath, but refused to drop her gaze from his as she whispered, "Because I was ashamed."

"Why, honey?" He could no longer keep from touching her, and almost of its own volition, his hand reached out to cup her cheek, his fingers moving compulsively, tenderly against the soft skin. "It wasn't your fault you married a man that was a bastard."

"I know. Intellectually, I know you're right," Lily drew a painful, deep breath. "But that doesn't change how I feel emotionally. I'm a well-educated, successful, mature woman, yet I allowed Derek to make my life a living hell. I can't help but be ashamed of my inability to get out before I did."

"You're being too hard on yourself, honey," Trace said softly, his heart twisting at the pain and shame in her eyes. "How old were you when you married him?"

"Nineteen."

"Nineteen," Trace mused, blue eyes narrowing in thought. "And you didn't date when you were in school? Just how many men had you dated before you met this slug?"

"One," Lily confessed. "A boy I toured with when I was fifteen."

"So you had little or no experience with men when you met your ex-husband," Trace concluded shrewdly.

"None to speak of, no," she admitted, her fingers twisting in the hem of the T-shirt.

Trace saw the telling movement and recognized the difficulty she still felt when talking about her marriage. He smoothed his palm down the side of her neck, his thumb stroking the line of her throat, and his fingers closed over the curve of her shoulder.

"We might as well get comfortable," he said softly, tugging her forward until she toppled against him. With easy movements, he tucked her against him, her smooth, bare legs resting along his larger, hair-roughened ones, her head tucked beneath his chin, and his arms wrapped around her while she rested her cheek against his bare chest. Comfort was only half of his aim. He shrewdly perceived that it would be easier for her to tell him her story if she didn't have to look at him while she was speaking. "Now, you only dated one other guy before, so how did you meet this jerk?"

He felt her smile against his bare skin and sighed with pleasure at the touch of her mouth against him and with relief that she was relaxed enough to be amused.

"My father introduced him to me," Lily said. "Derek approached my father to join him in an investment group. My father thought he was wonderful, and so did I, at first. He was older, charming, sophisticated, and seemed to be totally taken with me; he swept me off my feet. I was very naive. My father traveled with me and managed my career and, though I didn't realize it at the time, he managed my private life as well. I didn't really have a life of my own, I certainly had no friends or social life outside the friends he picked for me, and most of them were much older musicians or industry people whom I worked with."

"So your father encouraged the marriage?" Trace asked, wondering why the older man hadn't seen through Kenyon's veneer.

"Yes." Lily nodded her head, sending the silky hair sliding over his shoulder and arm and brushing against the underside of his chin. "He completely approved of Derek. Even after I told him about the woman in London, he told me that if Derek was seeking out other women, it must be because I wasn't doing all I could to please him."

"Wait a minute. What woman in London?" Trace asked.

"We took a honeymoon trip to London. I came home from shopping at Marks and Spencers three weeks after our wedding and walked in on him and another woman in bed."

"In *your* bed?" Trace was stunned.

"Yes," Lily acknowledged, her voice totally lacking in emotion.

"This guy really is a bastard," Trace muttered, his arms tightening around her.

Lily smoothed a soothing palm across the taut muscles of his bare chest.

"It was a long time ago, Trace; it hasn't mattered for a long time." She tilted her face back to meet his searching gaze. The outrage in his blue eyes faded and she returned her cheek to its resting place against his warm skin. "But it mattered then, a lot. I ran straight to my father's hotel—we were combining our honeymoon with a concert series I was doing in Europe. My mother died when I was twelve, so I didn't have a woman to turn to, only my father, and I believed him when he told me it was my fault."

"Your fault?!" Trace couldn't contain the explosion or the oath that accompanied it.

"You have to remember that I was very young, Trace, and I'd been very sheltered. And I have to confess that since I've known you, I think it may have been more my fault than I'm willing to admit."

"Why?" Trace frowned down at her. "What do you mean?"

"I never felt about Derek the way I feel about you. The way I feel *with* you. He never made my bones melt, his touch never made me want to rip his clothes off and attack him. And when he made love to me, it was uncomfortable at first and only got worse."

"Honey, you were a virgin, weren't you?" Trace asked, his palm moving under the knit T-shirt to her waist, where his fingers moved in absentminded, caressing circles against silky bare skin.

"Yes."

"And I'll bet he expected you to perform like someone with a lot of experience. He didn't take his time with you, did he?"

"No, I don't know—maybe not," she said slowly. "But even if he had, I don't think it would have helped. I just didn't want him the way I want you."

"I'm glad, honey." Trace's voice deepened, roughened with pleasure that what she felt for him was different and that she was willing to admit it. "But even if you didn't, he was older and probably a lot more experienced with sex than you were. He could have seduced you; the fact that you didn't enjoy it only tells me that he didn't bother to try."

"Hmm." Lily wasn't altogether convinced. But she *was* completely convinced that making love with Trace was nothing like the unpleasant encounters she'd had to endure with Derek.

"Is that why he started hitting you?" Trace prompted, relieved when the slim body pressed against his didn't stiffen.

"Yes," she admitted starkly. "At first it was because I didn't respond to him in bed the way he wanted, and because I didn't want to do some of the things he wanted me to do to him. But later, he had other women and he slept in another room. Then he started hitting me for any reason at all—because dinner wasn't hot enough, because I was late getting home from rehearsal—any excuse was enough to send him into a rage." She shuddered, and Trace's arms contracted, holding her tighter, safer. "He's a horrible man, Trace."

"You're right, sweetheart, he is," Trace agreed, his lips brushing the warm, silky crown of her head as he spoke. "Why didn't your father take you away from him when he saw what was happening?"

"My father never saw. I don't think he wanted to see," Lily said, and for the first time, raw hurt and betrayal invaded her voice. "He didn't believe me when I told him about the violence. Even when I told him that Derek admitted he only married me for the money, my father still wouldn't believe me. He told me that a divorce would create a scandal and hurt my career; it could cost us thousands. He told me again that it was my duty to please Derek, and that if he was seeing other women it was my fault for not satisfying him. He refused to believe that the bruises on my body were caused by Derek. When I finally left Derek, I didn't tell my father. I wrote him a letter and just disappeared."

"You just disappeared," Trace repeated slowly. "That's why the articles in the papers and trade magazines stopped suddenly five years ago. Because you dropped out of sight when you left him."

"Yes," She tipped her head back to look up at him. "How did you know that?"

"Because I had Mark run a check on you." Trace saw her eyes widen in surprise, but refused to apologize for his actions. "You were afraid of something and I suspected it was your ex-husband. You wouldn't, or couldn't, tell me about it, so I did some investigating of my own." His blue gaze met hers with direct honesty. "His finding you in CastleRock after all this time may well be because he tracked you through my inquiries. I'm sorry that it scared you, but I'm not sorry that he's here. It saves me the time and expense of going looking for him."

Lily met his gaze with grave consideration.

"I never wanted to see him again," she admitted slowly. "But I have to, one more time, to be free of him forever. I'm tired of running and hiding. I want to face him and be finished with him."

"Five years," Trace mused. "Where were you all that time? How did you live?"

"I worked at odd jobs—waitressing, clerical jobs, telephone survey work—anything I could find; and I never stayed long in one place. I moved all over the western United States, always in small towns where Derek would never think to look for me. And I never contacted any of the people I knew in the music industry for fear that Derek would find out where I was."

"Did you see your father during that time?"

Lily shook her head. "No, I never saw him. I telephoned him once, but Derek had convinced him that I left him because I was doing drugs and that he tried to stop me. My father believed him; he refused to see me unless I was willing to return to Derek and undergo psychiatric testing, and he froze my trust fund money so I didn't have access to it."

Trace bit back an oath. No wonder she trusted men so little. The very men she should have been able to rely on had let her down in the cruelest, most basic of ways.

"Do you want to see him?" he managed to ask calmly.

"No," she said in a small voice. "At least not now. Maybe someday, but not right away."

"Okay, honey," Trace said huskily. "You don't have to do anything you don't want to, all right?"

"All right," she sighed and snuggled closer. Beneath her cheek, his heart pounded in a strong, steady beat beneath sleek muscles.

Trace held her close, thinking about all that she'd told him.

"The music," he said thoughtfully, his fingers sifting through her hair. "You told me once that bad things happened to you and the music stopped playing. Was it your marriage and Derek that were the 'bad things'?"

"Yes." Once again, Lily's voice held a sad trace of sorrow. "The worse my life with Derek became, the less I heard the music, and that only made him angrier and more violent, because it lessened the amount of income I was able to generate."

Trace reflected grimly that Lily's ex-husband had a great deal to answer for and he would take great pleasure in exacting payment.

"But that doesn't matter anymore." Lily shed the brief sadness, her voice even huskier as she turned liquid lavender eyes up to his. "Because you gave me love and brought the music back."

Trace felt such a surge of overpowering emotion that for a moment he couldn't speak.

"Tell me you love me," he said hoarsely, his big body

clenching in an agony of suspense while he waited for her reply.

"I love you," she whispered.

And Trace dropped his mouth to hers in a kiss that held promises, sealed vows, and slowly changed from sweet, fervent renewals to heated passion.

# ELEVEN

''Make love to me, Trace, I need you,'' Lily whispered against his mouth.

Trace's fingers tightened against her scalp; he wanted her desperately but the smoky lavender eyes that met his had faint dark shadows beneath them, and her face was pale beneath the flush of desire that stroked across her cheekbones.

''I want to, baby,'' he said huskily, clamping down ruthlessly on the need that urged him to give her what she wanted and what he so desperately needed. ''I need you, too. You'll never know how much, but you're exhausted.'' He smoothed a fingertip over the shadow beneath her eye. ''If I didn't know it was impossible,'' he teased softly, ''I'd think you missed me almost as much as I missed you.''

''More,'' she said, closing her eyes as his fingertip traced her brows and the line of her nose. ''I missed you more. I haven't slept at all since you walked out of my house.''

''Then we'll both sleep tonight.'' Trace's mouth tilted

in a tender smile as her eyes flew open in protest. "But I'm going to wake you up *very* early in the morning."

He shifted them lower in the bed, and leaned over to snap off the bedside lamp, throwing the room into darkness, before he pulled the sheet and comforter up and tucked them around Lily's shoulders.

"Comfortable?" he asked as she made small, settling movements against his chest.

"Uhmm, very," Lily said drowsily, nuzzling her cheek against the sculpted muscles she lay against. Exhausted by the weeks with little sleep and strained emotions, she quickly fell asleep.

Trace lay awake, knowing by the soft, even rise and fall of her breasts snugged against his chest the very moment that she gave in to slumber, her body going relaxed and boneless where it lay against his. Even in sleep, her arms and hands clung to him as if she were afraid to let him go. His own arms tightened around her body in an instinctively possessive movement. No matter what happened tomorrow, he wasn't giving her up. Married or not, she belonged to him.

Lily was having the most wonderful dream. Warm, calloused palms smoothed over her back and down her thigh before reversing direction to glide with slow strokes over the flatness of her belly, the small indentation of her navel, and up over her rib cage to cup the taut, swelling curve of her breast. She sighed, arching her back to push against the caressing hand, her nipple nudging the warm palm when it obligingly lingered to fondle the tightening peak.

"Trace?" she asked huskily, still half asleep, her eyes still closed to better absorb the warm, sure touch that was sending rivulets of heated pleasure coursing through her veins to pool low in her belly.

"I'm here, sweetheart," he murmured against her

throat, where his lips had joined his hands in exploring the silky skin. He'd awakened disoriented and, at first, he thought he was dreaming again, but it didn't take long to realize that the warm, silky body in his arms really was Lily. His sleepy exploration quickly turned to hot intentness, and when she turned in his arms and slid her arms around his neck, her fingers threading through the tawny thickness of his hair to tug his mouth gently up to meet hers, he was fully aroused.

Trace rolled her onto her back, his weight half blanketing her and Lily sighed with pleasure. His arousal nudged her thigh, and her body turned liquid with anticipation.

Deaf to anything but each other's sighs and groans of pleasure, the loud pounding on the door downstairs went on for several moments before either of them heard the sound.

Trace lifted his head and dragged air into his lungs, trying to concentrate over the loud pounding of his heart.

"What is it?" Lily murmured, her palms continuing their compulsive stroking down the line of his back.

Trace frowned as he realized that the pounding wasn't just the sound of his heart.

"Somebody's at the door," he growled.

"Ignore them, maybe they'll go away," Lily whispered, and leaned up to explore the throbbing pulse at the base of his neck with damp, warm lips.

Trace's eyes slid closed, his hands clenching over the sheet at the sheer pleasure of her mouth moving against his skin. Her tongue ventured out to taste him in tentative, shy strokes, and he jerked in reaction. He stood the exquisite torture as long as he could before he fastened his hands in her hair and turned her face up to bury his lips against hers, his tongue moving into the warm, wet hollow of her mouth, echoing the movements of his hips against hers.

Slowly, the knocking sound penetrated his absorption again and, in frustration, he lifted his head and looked down at Lily's flushed, passion-drowsy face.

"Somebody's damn determined to reach me," he said, brushing a kiss against her softly swollen mouth. "I'll get rid of them."

He threw back the comforter and stood, pulling on a pair of jeans with quick, impatient movements before he left the room.

He yanked open the front door and glowered at Jesse, who stood on the front porch with his fist raised to knock again.

"What do you want?" he snarled with irritation.

Jesse's startled green gaze swept Trace's glowering features, not missing the tousled blond hair, before moving down over his bare chest and the unbuttoned Levi's to his bare feet before swiftly returning to meet his blue gaze.

"Uh-oh," he said with dawning realization. "Am I interrupting something?"

"Yes, damn it," Trace bit out. "Now what the hell is so important that you have to pound my door down?"

"Is Lily here?" Jesse countered.

"What if she is?"

"If she is, I have some important news for her."

"Like what?"

"Like her husband's in town looking for her."

Trace's body went tense, his expression changing swiftly from irritation to menace.

"Where?"

"At her house. Sarah and I dropped by there this morning. Sarah tried to reach her by phone, and when she couldn't get an answer, she fretted about it until I ran her by the house. When we knocked, a man answered the door and told us he was Lily's husband and that he was waiting for her. He didn't know where she was, but I figured if she wasn't at her house, then the only other place she could be was here.''

Trace's eyes narrowed murderously.

''Arrogant son of a bitch,'' he ground out. ''After all these years, he thinks he can just romp back into her life and walk into her house without her permission.''

''Did you already know he was in town?'' Jesse asked, reading only anger but no surprise in Trace's reaction.

''Yeah. Come on in.'' He turned away and Jesse stepped into the house, following Trace as he stalked through the living room and into the kitchen. Trace was measuring coffee into the coffee maker. ''We left the Lakeshore last night and went to her house; he'd been there, and from the looks of the dirty cups and the mess he made, he'd probably waited for quite a while. He left Lily a note.'' He switched the coffee maker on with a savage movement and thrust the fingers of one hand through his hair before folding his arms across his chest and leaning his hips against the counter. The planes of his face went hard with restrained violence. ''You should have seen her face when she read his signature. She panicked, and started running around throwing clothes into suitcases. She was damn near hysterical. She was incapable of being rational, and she wouldn't listen to me until I finally grabbed her and held her still. Whatever he did to her, it must have been bad. She's scared to death of him.''

Jesse's features had stiffened as he listened, his green eyes going cold and purposeful.

''She won't be when we get done with him,'' he said with grim sureness.

''We can't do that, Jesse.''

''Why not?'' Jesse stared at his best friend as if he'd

taken leave of his senses. ''Don't tell me you don't want to rearrange this guy's face, because I don't believe it.''

''You know me better than that.'' Trace's somber gaze met Jesse's. ''I'd like nothing more than to show him how it feels to be the one on the receiving end of a beating. But Lily has to face him herself.''

''Why?'' The single word burst from a disbelieving Jesse.

''Because she needs to face him. She's run from him so long that he's grown to be an enormous, threatening monster in her mind. It's important—to her pride in herself and her own peace of mind—that she face him and tell him he's no longer a threat and that she's no longer afraid of him.''

Jesse's dark-haired head nodded in reluctant understanding. Still, it went against his every protective instinct to let Lily walk into danger.

''But you're going to be there with her, right?''

Trace sent him a disgusted, hot-blue glance.

''Of course I am. And I hope to God he tries something, anything, so I have an excuse to throw him out the front door!''

''Good.'' Jesse nodded in satisfied approval. ''Just for added security, I think I'll arrange for Mark to escort him out of town. He'll enjoy that.''

''Yeah.'' For the first time, Trace's lips curled in a brief, appreciative grin. ''He would.''

''I'll go arrange it.'' Jesse pushed away from the doorframe he leaned against. ''You'll be at Lily's house?''

''Right. I take it Kenyon planned to wait for her there?''

''Far as I could tell; he seemed to have made himself at home. He was drinking coffee when he answered the door.''

''We'll be there,'' Trace said grimly. ''Give us an hour to shower, dress, and drive over.''

"I'll be there, too." Anticipation curled Jesse's mouth in a wolfish grin. "And so will Mark."

Trace heard the front door click shut after Jesse before he turned and pulled open the cabinet doors above the counter to the left of the sink to take down two mugs. He poured them full of hot black coffee and climbed the stairs, his bare feet making no sound on the treads. He paused in the doorway of his bedroom. Unconsciously graceful, Lily lay sprawled on her back in the center of the bed, the sheet tucked over her breasts, her arms bent upward with hands lying palms-up against the pillows. Her hair made a fan of black silk against the stark white of the pillowcases, and her face was turned away from him to the window, where pale winter sunshine poured through the panes.

Lily lay, quietly sleepy, gazing out the window and waiting for Trace, wondering idly what was taking him so long and who had been at the door. Outside the window, the bare branch of a birch tree was silhouetted against the wintry sky, the tree swaying in the little gusts of wind that rubbed its rough bark in an oddly soothing, rhythmic, scritch-scratch against the cold glass pane.

She didn't hear a sound, but the tantalizing scent of coffee tickled her nose, and she turned her head on the pillow to find Trace standing in the doorway watching her.

"Hi," she said softly, lavender eyes warm as they moved over his face. He was holding two steaming mugs in his hands. "Is that what took you so long?" she asked curiously, rolling to face him and propping her cheek on her fist. "You were making coffee?"

Trace read the questioning confusion on her face and in her violet eyes.

"That was part of it," he admitted, walking to the bed and handing her one of the cups of steaming brew before he bent a knee and sat down on the bed beside her.

Something was wrong. Lily sensed it in the tension that emanated from his taut body, she could see it in the dark, concerned blue gaze that stroked over her face.

"Part of it?" She sipped the coffee, grateful for the caffeine that she knew would chase the cobwebs from her admittedly fuzzy, not-quite-awake-yet brain.

"Jesse was at the door," he said, not really answering her question.

"Oh? What did he want?"

"He and Sarah stopped by your house this morning," Trace saw the inadvertent tightening of her fingers over the handle of the mug, and silently cursed Derek Kenyon. "Kenyon was there."

Lily slowly lowered the mug of coffee until it rested on the bed. Unwavering, her violet gaze held his.

"Did they talk to him," she asked.

"Yes, he said he was waiting for you."

"Well, then," she said, and with cool aplomb gracefully sat up in bed without spilling her coffee or losing the sheet she held to her breasts, "I suppose we should get dressed."

A fierce surge of pride rocked him.

"You don't need to be afraid, Lily," he said, his deep tones reassuring. "He isn't going to hurt you."

"I know." The lavender gaze she raised to his held an unwavering trust that staggered him. "I should have realized long ago that I can trust you. I'm not afraid of him anymore, Trace, not deep down."

"I'm glad, baby." His deep voice was rough with emotion and pride in the bravery that tilted her chin and reflected calmly in the depths of her eyes. He cleared his throat. "You can have the shower first. I'd like to share, but we wouldn't get out of here for hours and I want this over and done with and Kenyon out of CastleRock."

Lily's eyes widened at the thought of showering with him.

Trace saw the arrested interest in her expression and groaned before he rolled to his feet.

"Stop that! I'm doing my damnedest to keep my hands to myself, but I'll never make it if you keep looking at me like that!"

"Like what?" Lily asked innocently, her mouth curving in a completely female smile.

"Like that." He bent swiftly and pressed a kiss against that teasing smile, groaning with frustration when he reluctantly ripped his mouth from her clinging lips. "Get in the shower. I'm going downstairs, out of temptation's reach, and make us breakfast."

"Chicken," Lily called softly after his disappearing back.

"Damned straight!" he threw over his shoulder before loping down the stairs.

She sighed, and carefully balancing the cooling mug of coffee, threw back the sheet and got out of bed. She dreaded the coming confrontation with Derek, but no longer was she paralyzed with fear. Knowing that Trace would be with her removed her physical fear, and the emotional support he provided made her resolve only that much stronger. Purposefully, she headed for the bathroom and a shower. Like Trace, she, too, wanted the coming confrontation over and done with and Derek banished out of her life forever.

Trace was standing in front of the mirror shaving when she pushed back the shower curtain. His gaze shifted in the steamy mirror from his foam-covered cheeks and chin to her towel-wrapped figure, his hand stilling the razor's sweeping strokes that had already left the right side of his face bare. With an effort, he yanked his gaze away from her flushed cheeks below the tumble of black silk that threatened to escape the pins holding it piled loosely atop her head and the bare curve of her shoulders above the wrapped towel that clung precariously to the swell of her breasts. He frowned fiercely at his reflection in the mirror and concentrated on methodically scraping the razor along the line of his jaw.

Lily watched him in fascination for a long moment before she walked up behind him and wrapped her arms around his waist to hug him, her cheek lying against his shoulder blade.

"I love watching you shave."

"Oh, yeah?" He glanced back over his shoulder, stomach muscles twitching with surges of pleasure at the clasp of small, soft hands against his bare skin. "What's so great about it?"

"I don't know, it's such a—a male sort of thing. I like it," she said simply, tilting her head sideways so her gaze could meet his. His eyes darkened. "I like that, too," she said, a slow smile tilting her mouth while her fingertips moved in delicate, testing strokes around the hollow of his navel.

"What?" he managed to get out, his deep voice gravelly.

"The way your eyes get dark and sexy when you look at me," she whispered. "Like they do when we're making love."

Trace groaned and twisted around, catching her against him and bending to take her mouth with his in one swift movement. Separated by only the damp towel and his jeans, smooth skin moved against sleek muscles with seductive strokes that soon had them both burning with a furnace heat.

His heart racing, Trace forced himself to lift his mouth from hers, his arms tightening to press her against him in a vain effort to pull her inside his skin.

"Damn," he breathed, his chest lifting and falling as he drew in shuddering lungsful of air. "We've got to stop this. We don't have time for hours of making love." Holding her in the circle of his arms, he tipped his head back to look down at her, and a grin spread across his face. One calloused fingertip trailed across her cheek, and he held it up in front of her still-dazed eyes. It was covered with white foam. "I think you've got more of my shaving cream on your face than I have on mine."

"Oh!" Lily nudged him aside and looked in the mirror. White shaving cream was smudged on her cheek and one earlobe and across the tip of her nose. She caught up his towel from the countertop and made a face at his reflection watching her in the mirror. "You should be ashamed of yourself," she said with mock severity. "Taking advantage of me like that."

"Yeah, ri-i-ight," he drawled, narrowing his eyes threateningly. She calmly ignored him and he closed his palms over the smooth curves of her shoulders and shifted her to the left and away from the mirror. "Go get dressed, woman, or I'll show you *taking advantage*."

Lily laughed and collected her underclothes from the top of the wicker hamper and her dress from the brass hook on the back of the door, lingering just long enough to see him start to shave again before she left to dress.

"How you doin'? Okay?" Trace glanced sideways and reached out to take her cold hand in his. The interior of the Camaro was comfortably warm, and he knew her cold fingers weren't caused by the chill wintry day.

"Fine," Lily mustered a small smile, but her fingers tightened on his. "I'm glad you're with me," she added, sending him a sideways glance from between thick lashes.

"I'll always be with you," he answered, his calm voice carrying a declaration of intent that allowed no argument.

Lily was more than grateful for his staunch, steady support. Even though, backed by Trace's physical strength, she truly wasn't afraid of Derek, still the impending encounter was bound to be ugly. Knowing Derek as she did, she had no illusion that he would gracefully accept her decision not to have anything more to do with him.

Trace turned the Camaro onto her street and nudged it into the curb behind a Buick with rental car plates on its bumper.

"Looks like he's still here," he commented tersely.

"Yes," Lily said starkly.

Trace gave her hand a last, encouraging squeeze and got out of the car. He handed her out with care, his hand beneath her elbow as they walked side by side up the snowy walk and climbed the porch. Trace glanced down the street just in time to see Mark's black-and-white cruiser turn the corner. He nodded his head in brusque response to Jesse's wave from the passenger seat, and then focused all his attention on the opening door.

The man seated on the sofa watching television, his legs propped on top of the coffee table, looked up when the door moved inward. Trace didn't miss the brief spurt of anticipated victory when he saw Lily, nor the quick flash of calculating cunning when his gaze flicked to include her companion.

Derek Kenyon rose gracefully to his feet. Just under six feet tall, his cream turtleneck beneath a camel-colored cashmere sweater paired beautifully with caramel wool slacks, and together with his black hair, St.-Tropez tan, and perfect white teeth, he created a picture of expensive elegance.

"Lily! At last." He moved toward her, hands held out to take hers.

Lily took an instinctive step backward and came up against Trace's solid, familiar bulk.

"What are you doing here, Derek?" she asked in a commendably calm voice.

His smooth features looked wounded, perfect white teeth gleaming in a falsely conciliatory smile.

"Darling, where else should I be? When I found you . . . after many long years of searching," he added, with a gentle, admonishing look, "I was appalled to find you living in these tawdry surroundings, your talent being wasted in a meaningless public school and teaching grubby students. Of course, I flew to you as quickly as I could to take you away from all this."

"I'm afraid your flight was wasted." Lily's voice held a touch of irony in appreciation of his theatrics. "I have absolutely no desire to leave CastleRock."

"Of course you do, Lily," he said smoothly, ignoring her words. "When I told Pacific Theatrical Management that you were available again, they were very interested. They already have you booked for eight dates on the East Coast."

Lily's eyes flashed lavender fire.

"Then they'll just have to cancel them. I'm not leaving CastleRock."

"You're not thinking clearly." Derek's voice displayed barely a trace of the irritation that flushed his cheeks beneath his carefully cultivated tan. "You can't possibly want to stay in this one-horse town. There's nothing here for you."

"There's everything here," Lily said with firm conviction. "And absolutely nothing that I want in L.A."

Derek's brown eyes narrowed suspiciously, and his gaze flicked to Trace's set features.

"What's here for you?" he asked, faint ridicule underlying his smooth tones.

"My work, my friends." Lily didn't hesitate, her gaze

meeting his without wavering. "The man I'm going to marry."

Again, Derek's gaze flicked to Trace before returning to Lily.

"Him?" he asked, a sneer underlying the word.

Trace's muscles clenched, and he strained against the self-imposed bonds that kept him from shifting Lily aside and wiping the sneer off the other man's well-tended face.

"Yes," Lily answered. Alert to every subtle shift of Trace's big body at her back, she knew the effort it cost him not to interfere.

"Even supposing I believed you're serious about this—person," he said insultingly, pausing to run a derisive gaze over Trace. "It's going to be a little bit difficult to marry him, considering you're already married to me."

"That can be taken care of. Divorces are fairly easy to get."

Derek eyed her consideringly. This wasn't the same naive little girl who had been so easily intimidated five years ago. Gone was the girl. In her place was a woman of purpose. Playing the role of concerned father-figure was clearly not working, and he decided to change his tactics.

"Darling . . ." His voice softened cajolingly. "I know I made mistakes and that our marriage wasn't the best of relationships, but surely we can try again? We're both older, and I'm deeply regretful for anything I did that hurt you. Marriage is a sacred union, we can't just turn our backs on it without giving it every chance."

Lily stared at him. It was difficult to believe that the smooth-talking, tanned charmer standing in front of her had ever convinced her that he was sincere. He changed like a chameleon before her eyes, switching his approach like a snake sheds skins as he probed for a weakness.

"I agree, Derek," she said slowly.

Trace went taut and still at her back. Derek smiled, a small, assured, vindictive smile of victory.

"I agree that marriage is a sacred union and that when two people join their lives, it should be for life. That kind of marriage is what I know I can have with Trace, and what I could never have with you."

Derek lost any vestige of politeness or supplication. His thin lips drew back in a feral snarl, his face going ugly with viciousness. He lifted his hand in an instinctive need to strike, and Trace moved swiftly, stepping in front of Lily with a fluid movement.

"Try it, Kenyon . . ." His voice was a low, lethal purr of invitation. "Just once."

Derek halted, going instantly still as he realized that he'd badly underestimated the man who now stood only a few feet from him. He was within easy reach of Trace's rock-hard body and his fists that opened and closed in mute testimony to the fury that strained to slip its leash.

"This is between me and my wife," he said, the bravado he injected in his voice slipping a notch.

"You're wrong," Trace snarled, his eyes silver ice over hot blue fire. "You changed the rules the minute you threatened her."

"I didn't threaten her," Derek blustered, taking a step backward. "Any man would understandably be upset to hear his wife say she's planning to marry another man!"

Lily's fingers closed over Trace's forearm.

"Please, Trace, I don't want any violence," she said softly.

"There's no reason to get physical," Derek agreed quickly, his brown gaze darting between Lily's worried features and Trace's lethal glare. His lashes narrowed over calculating eyes as he considered the depth of Lily's willingness to avoid unpleasantness. "I can see that you've made up your mind, Lily, and that you're determined to follow this course. Even though I can't approve, I'm willing to step aside and bow to your wishes.''

''I appreciate that, Derek,'' Lily said, wondering what lay beneath his sudden willingness to cooperate.

''Of course, California property laws being what they are, the legal entanglements may drag on for a number of years,'' he added with pseudoconcern.

''Really?'' Lily was beginning to get an inkling as to where this conversation was going.

''Oh, yes.'' Derek shook his head with regret. He shot a sideways glance at Trace, and was relieved to find that the big man now stood with arms folded across his broad chest, his face unreadable except for an alert, threatening blue gaze that flicked from Lily's face to his. ''There are ways to avoid a lengthy litigation, as I'm sure you are aware.''

''I'm afraid I'm not,'' Lily responded, anticipating his response.

''Well, we can arrange a financial settlement privately, just between the two of us, without the courts being involved. Then the divorce itself is just a formality.''

''Really?'' Trace interjected, his voice deceptively mild. ''Just how much of a settlement did you have in mind?''

Derek named a sum that was so high, Lily could only blink in shock. Trace glanced at her face and then back at Derek.

''I don't think so,'' he said, his calm voice belied by the feral smile that curved his mouth. ''Lily isn't giving you a dime, Kenyon. She's already paid by having to live with you during your short marriage.''

''Are you going to let your bodyguard speak for you?'' Derek asked, barely able to keep his fury from coloring his voice.

Lily glanced from Derek's livid face to Trace's blue gaze, before she answered.

"Yes," she said calmly, her lavender gaze meeting Derek's furious one with no trace of fear. "I am."

Stymied on all fronts, Derek struggled to hold on to his volatile, explosive temper. A struggle that he lost.

"You're a fool," he ground out. "You'll never be able to get married again. I'll keep us tied up in California courts for years!"

"Then I'll just live with Trace," Lily said, sliding her hand into Trace's and stepping closer.

"You?!" He laughed, a vicious, sneering sound. "The original prude? I doubt it!"

"She won't have to," Trace said, watching Derek like a cat with a mouse, "because you've been married twice in the five years since Lily left you. If you drag your feet about the divorce, we'll make sure you're arrested for bigamy."

Both Derek and Lily stared at Trace in shock.

"Is that true, Derek?" Lily whispered.

"It's true," Trace answered when Derek was silent. "When Mark ran a check on you, he also did a background check on Kenyon. He's been married and divorced twice in the last five years."

Caught in his web of lies, Derek had nothing to gain anymore.

"It's true that I've been married," he sneered sarcastically. "But your investigator did a poor job or he would have also discovered that I divorced Lily for desertion in Mexico."

"When?" She could hardly believe that all these years she had been legally free of him.

"A year after you left." His shoulders lifted in a dismissing shrug. "Your father finally got smart and cut off my access to your money. Stupid old man. Fortunately, I was seeing another, far richer woman who was more than eager to get married."

Kenyon's callous dismissal of events that had had such far-reaching, traumatic effect on Lily's life was the last straw. Trace glanced down at Lily's stunned face. "Do you have any more questions you want to ask him, or are you finished?" he asked her.

Still in shock from her ex-husband's revelations, Lily pulled her gaze away from Derek and found Trace watching her with keen concern.

"I'm finished," she managed to answer.

"Good," Trace said with satisfaction. He fastened eyes that glowed with grim purpose on the other man. "You're leaving. Now. And you're never, ever coming back. You're not even going to cross the Iowa state line. And if you even so much as see Lily in L.A. or anywhere else, you're going to immediately disappear. Do you understand?"

Derek glared at Trace.

"I understand." He got out grudgingly, before he turned and walked to the door.

Trace stalked several steps behind him.

Derek pulled open the door and paused, halfway through, to look back.

"You're getting a bad bargain, friend. She's lousy in bed."

He made it through the door and onto the front porch before Trace caught him. Lily heard the thump of Trace's boots on the wooden boards and then the unmistakable sound of fist meeting flesh before Derek roared with pain. She ran across the living room and pulled open the door to find Derek sprawled on his back in the snowy front yard. Blood trickled in a crimson trail from his nose, and he lifted shaky fingers to wipe it away, only succeeding in smearing it across his face.

"I'll have you arrested for assault!" he yelled, pushing himself to his elbows.

"I doubt that," Trace said with satisfaction, absentmindedly rubbing the scraped skin on the knuckles of his right hand. "You're trespassing. Not to mention the small matter of breaking and entering."

Across the street, the doors of the police car slammed and Mark and Jesse started across the snowy street toward them.

Derek pushed himself to his feet, swaying slightly while he cursed Trace and tried to wipe the dripping blood from his face.

"Here, here," Mark Daly admonished sharply. "That's no kind of language to be using in front of a lady."

"A lady?!" Derek snarled, and spat a foul description that had Trace starting down the porch steps toward him.

"Stay right where you are, Trace," Mark snapped, and took Derek's shoulder in a hard grip to shove him toward the street and his car. "I think it's time you left Castle-Rock, friend. And just to make sure, I'm going to give you an escort across the county line."

Lily stood two steps above Trace on the porch and watched the burly, uniformed Mark yank open the driver's door of Derek's car and stuff the man inside. He waited until Kenyon started the engine and pulled away from the curb before heading across the street to his own car.

"See you later, Trace," he called over his shoulder. "Gotta make sure our friend doesn't need a speeding ticket on his way out of town."

Jesse raised a hand in farewell and the two men got into Mark's car and made a U-turn to follow Derek.

Lily laid a hand on Trace's shoulder and he turned to look up at her.

"Did you know all this time that I was divorced?" she asked.

# TWELVE

Trace read the uncertainty in her eyes and the curve of her mouth and shook his head in quick rejection.

"Oh, no, honey, I would have told you immediately if I'd known. I thought he remarried without bothering to get a divorce from you," he hastened to reassure her. "I was glad that we had the threat of bigamy to hold over his head if he balked at the divorce, but I didn't tell you because I didn't think you needed further proof that Kenyon was slime."

"You're right about that," Lily agreed. "I'm surprised that I ever believed anything that man said." The little frown between her brows smoothed away, and a slow smile curved her mouth upward, her eyes taking on a glow. "I'm free, Trace. I'm not married to him, I'm free!"

She threw her arms around his neck and hugged him. He staggered from her exuberant assault and caught her against him, laughing as she peppered his face with kisses.

"Yeah, but you're not easy," he chuckled. "I can vouch for that!"

* * *

Sarah McFadden and Jesse Lee James's wedding day dawned clear and cold, with pale-yellow sunshine that glittered off the snow outside the brick church.

Lily nudged her car into a parking space in the nearly vacant lot serving Grace Lutheran Church and checked her watch.

"One-thirty," she murmured out loud. "Right on time."

She collected her purse, the plastic garment bag with Victoria's Garden imprinted in flowing gold script across the front, and a drawstring bag containing her shoes, makeup, and various curling irons, brushes, and hairspray, and hurried across the snowy lot and up the steps into the church.

As she pulled open the heavy door, she remembered with a brief smile the last time she'd walked through these doors for the wedding rehearsal only a few days before. Then her feet had dragged in time with her heartbeat as she reluctantly dreaded seeing Trace inside the church. Now her steps were buoyant, her heart light as she anticipated the coming wedding.

She stepped into the foyer and followed the sound of women's voices down the stairs to the basement. Here, a Sunday school classroom had been commandeered to serve as a dressing room. Lily pushed open the door and walked into organized chaos. The bridesmaids were in various stages of undress, chattering and laughing as they curled each other's hair and closed zippers. Their Christmas-red-and-green dresses billowed on hangers hooked over window frames. Mirrors were propped against one wall, and the little flower girl, Stacy, her long hair in fat sausage curls that fell down her back, posed and pirouetted in front of the glass. Lily worked her way through the crowded room to the far side where Sarah sat, dressed in a short silk kimono over a merry widow, matching slip, and cobwebby hose, a blue garter around her thigh above her knee, while Melanie Winters touched up her hair with a curling iron.

Head bent forward while Melanie worked, Sarah watched Lily approach in the mirror.

"Hi, I'm glad you're here. I wasn't sure Trace would let you out of his sight long enough for you to get dressed," she teased, blue eyes sparkling.

Lily blushed becomingly, still unused to references to her relationship with Trace.

"He drove over to pick up Jesse when I left the house to come here," she said calmly, feeling the heat in her cheeks.

"Oh, good." As usual, Sarah was instantly diverted by her fiancé's name. "Was Trace already dressed when he left?"

"Yes." Lily's face took on a dreamy expression. "Why is it men look so incredible in a tuxedo?"

"I don't know." Sarah laughed. "Actually, Jesse looks pretty good in jeans, too."

"So does Trace." The two exchanged glances and laughed.

"If you two don't stop drooling over your men and get dressed, you're going to be late for the wedding," Melanie commented dryly, tucking a final curl into the blond cluster on top of Sarah's head.

"You're right, Melanie." Sarah peered into the mirror, turning her head from side to side. "That's perfect! I don't know how I managed to lose pins just driving from the beauty shop to the church!"

"I don't, either." Melanie smiled with amusement. Sarah was so wired, she positively glowed with excitement. "Do you want me to help you with your dress?"

"Yes, please. Mom was going to be here, but it must

have taken her longer than she expected to get Daddy into his tuxedo and tie.''

Lily hung her dress over the back of a chair and piled her other belongings next to the mirror before stripping off her coat, sweater, and jeans. Beneath them, she wore a pink merry widow, bikini panties, and hose required for the crimson velvet bridesmaid's gown. She untied the loose knot in the bottom of the plastic garment bag and slipped it upward to free her dress from its hanger. Carefully stepping into the skirt, she pulled the gown up over her hips and pushed her hands through the close-fitting sleeves before pulling the scoop-necked bodice up over her shoulders.

''Need some help with the zipper, Lily?'' Melanie asked.

''Yes, please.'' Lily gathered the thick mane of her hair into an ebony sheaf and pulled it forward while Melanie deftly eased the zipper closed and fastened the tiny hook-and-eye closure at the top. Lily tossed her hair back over her shoulder and looked at her reflection in the mirror before her gaze moved to Melanie's green-eyed reflection. ''The dresses are absolutely beautiful, Melanie, and they fit perfectly.''

''Thank you.'' The designer's answer reflected a quiet pride. ''Wedding gowns and bridesmaids dresses are my favorite gowns to design. And my creations always look twice as good because the people who wear them are so happy and excited,'' she laughed softly. ''Sometimes I think I could dress a wedding party in gunny sacks with flowers and they would look wonderful! There's just something about a wedding . . .''

''Not all weddings,'' Lily said in a neutral tone, her eyes taking on a faraway look as she remembered the hurried civil ceremony that had joined her life to Derek's. Deliberately, she banished the memory. She refused to let bad memories spoil this day. "But this one will definitely be something wonderful."

"Absolutely!" Jeannie McFadden, hurrying toward Sarah, overheard Lily's comment and smiled at Lily and Melanie. "If we can just get the men through it without them ripping off their ties and unbuttoning their collars."

"Hi, Mom, where have you been?"

"I was forcing your father to get dressed and retieing his tie, at least a *dozen* times," Jeannie answered, and then stopped abruptly to stare at her daughter in the lace-and-satin wedding dress. "Oh, Sarah," she said, gray eyes misting with emotion. "You're so beautiful."

Lily and Melanie diplomatically turned away to give mother and daughter a moment alone.

"That's quite a crowd out there, Jesse," Trace commented, peering over his best friend's shoulder and into the sanctuary through the crack created by Jesse's holding open the door. Located at the front of the church, just to the right of the altar and almost hidden behind the giant, ceiling-high Christmas tree that took up the corner between the front pew and the altar, it gave the two a perfect view of the packed church.

The wooden church pews on both sides of the crimson carpet that divided the guests of the bride and groom were nearly filled to capacity with relatives and friends of the young couple. The cheerful crowd chatted and laughed, some greeting familiar faces they hadn't seen since the last family celebration.

"Yeah," Jesse muttered, running a finger around his neck beneath his collar. "If it wasn't for Sarah, I wouldn't be caught dead going through this; I would have eloped."

Trace chuckled and clapped a sympathetic hand on Jesse's shoulder.

"Yeah, but she's worth it."

"True, she's worth it," Jesse repeated with conviction. He glanced over his shoulder at Trace. "When are you and Lily getting married?"

"Just as soon as I can talk her into it. I think she's still trying to absorb the fact that she *isn't* married. I'm trying to give her a little time to get used to the idea, so I haven't said anything, but I'm running low on patience."

"Getting nervous, gentlemen?" Pastor Larson's quiet voice behind them brought both men turning quickly to face him. He smiled benignly at their guilty faces. "It's all right, I haven't had a groom and best man yet who hasn't peeked through that door."

Trace and Jesse exchanged sheepish glances.

"Well, then." The pastor adjusted his glasses and smoothed his gold-embroidered crimson stole over his snowy white surplice. "I think the ladies are ready, and we don't want to keep the bride waiting, now do we?"

"No," Jesse answered, the smile that lit his face filled with heartfelt emotion. "No, we don't."

"Very well, gentlemen, follow me." Pastor Larson pulled open the door and walked with measured tread into the sanctuary, where he climbed the three shallow steps and turned to face the expectant crowd.

Jesse and Trace obediently followed him, and halted at the foot of the steps, turning to look down the long crimson-covered aisle to the back of the church.

It was Jesse's wedding day, but Trace knew his friend couldn't feel any more anxious than he did. His blue gaze focused with fierce intensity on the doorway, Trace felt a surge of relief when the first strains of the wedding march sounded from the choir loft, and little Stacy Wilson stepped into the doorway. The wedding guests surged to their feet, turning to face the back of the church with expectant faces. The ladies oohed and aahed over the picture of innocence created by Stacy's long blond curls against floor-length red velvet as she walked carefully down the aisle, tossing white rose petals against the red carpet.

Trace barely glanced at the little girl except to register that, at last, the wedding had started and soon, very soon, his Lily would be walking through the door. Impatiently, he counted two bridesmaids and then he caught his breath, his heart stopping before shuddering into a fast, thundering beat.

Lily stepped into the doorway and took Mark's arm, her fingers tightening over his sleeve as her searching gaze found Trace. Standing at Jesse's left, elegant in a black tuxedo, his gaze blazed with blue fire when he saw her. She felt an answering leap of her own heart, and, mesmerized by the love and pride on his handsome face, she floated down the aisle toward him.

Trace managed to rip his gaze from Lily to watch Sarah walk down the aisle on his father's arm, and easily recognized the love on Jesse's face when he took Sarah's hand from Gavin and drew her forward to kneel in front of the altar. His gaze flicked to Lily and found her watching him with tears in her eyes, the love she felt for him unhidden, glowing deep in misty lavender eyes, as if a candle had been lit within her.

Lily listened as Pastor Larson spoke, his brief sermon on the sanctity of the wedding vows striking a deep chord within her.

*Yes*, she thought with deep certainty. *This is what I want with Trace. I need his Sunday kind of love as much as he does.*

"Repeat after me . . ." Pastor Larson said, his words breaking into her thoughts. "I, Jesse Lee James, take this woman, Sarah Anne McFadden . . ."

*I, Trace McFadden, take this woman, Lily Townsend,*

Trace said silently, his blue gaze fastened intently on Lily's.

". . . to love, and to cherish, from this day forward . . ."

*. . . to love and to cherish,* he thought. *Please, God, I will, forever, from this day forward.*

"And do you Sarah Anne McFadden, take this man, Jesse Lee James . . ."

*I, Lily Townsend, take this man, Trace McFadden,* Lily's heart repeated.

". . . to love, and to cherish, from this day forward . . ."

*Yes, from this day forward, forever and ever, amen.*

Trace saw the barely perceptible movements of her lips and read the words in her eyes. With iron control he managed, just barely, to keep from crossing the short space of crimson carpet that separated them and crushing her in his arms.

Stunned by the intensity of emotion, somehow both Lily and Trace managed to walk through the rest of the ceremony, and when at last they met in the vestibule, Trace maneuvered her into a corner.

"Mark and I are switching partners for the rest of the day—I get you and he gets Angela."

"Good." Lily smiled up at him. "That makes me happy. How do Mark and Angela feel about that?"

"Mark's delighted, but I'm going to get a lot of flack from Josh." Trace grinned and slipped an arm around her shoulder as he turned to answer a question from his great aunt Trudy.

The Lakeshore Supper Club's owner was a longtime friend of the McFaddens and had pulled out all stops for the reception. Trace and Lily joined the rest of the wedding party, exchanging toasts and laughter.

Lily stood chatting with Trace and Gavin near the long French doors, closed tightly against the winter cold and the frozen lake outside, when Nathan McFadden joined them. His tall, spare form was elegant in a black suit and his blue eyes twinkled with humor.

"Well, Gavin, it's about time you married off one of these kids," he said jovially.

"You're right," Gavin agreed. "Now if I can just get the boys to follow their sister's example, maybe I'll have a few grandkids to bounce on my knee."

Trace lifted a meaningful eyebrow at Lily and she blushed, delicate pink color moving up her throat and across her cheekbones.

She sipped her glass of champagne and listened to the three talk.

"Who's the young man you brought with you, Nathan?" Gavin asked with curiosity, staring across the room. The young man he referred to leaned a shoulder against the wall, a champagne glass dangling from his fingers, his ice-blue gaze remote as he watched the dancers. Thick blond hair hung to his shoulders and a silver earring studded one ear. He wore a dark suit coat with the sleeves rolled up and a white shirt with no tie. The suit coat and the white shirt were his only concessions to formal wear, for Levi's covered his long legs and black cowboy boots his feet.

Nathan's sharp blue gaze followed Gavin's and found the young man.

"That's my great-nephew, Nicholas, Katherine's son, from California. Los Angeles, actually. He's twenty-four, just finished college, and he's on his way to Europe, danged if I know why. I told him he should see the United States, first, but I guess he's bummed all over the States on his motorcycle, working during summer vacations from school."

Nicholas's gaze drifted over the crowded room, and Nathan caught his eye, beckoning to him imperiously. He lifted his chin in acknowledgment and pushed away from the wall to wend his way through the crowd toward them.

"You McFaddens certainly breed true," she murmured to Trace as she watched the young man approach. "Look at that blond hair, and those cheekbones and blue eyes! You all look like Vikings!"

Trace, his back to the other two men and his head bent to catch her words, looked into her eyes and couldn't prevent the grin of pure deviltry that curved his mouth.

"Yeah, but you like Vikings, don't you?"

Lily stared at him; there was something familiar about his words. Vikings. Vikings?

He leaned closer and brushed a quick kiss against her mouth.

"Do you remember?"

Lily's thick lashes widened, violet eyes rounding as she remembered kissing him in the hospital. Oh, how she remembered!

"Oh, no," she said, flushing with mortification. "Tell me I didn't do that?"

"Do what?" Trace asked, blue eyes laughing down at her.

"You know what!" She glanced quickly around to be sure no one could hear her before she whispered in his ear, "Did I really grab you in the hospital and kiss you?"

"Yup, you sure did," he confirmed with obvious enjoyment. "And I loved every minute of it!"

"I didn't even know you!" She pressed her forehead against the black tuxedo covering his upper arm and groaned with embarrassment.

"I didn't know you, either," Trace said, his voice deepening. "But I was already in love with you."

Lily lifted her head and looked at him, awed by the love that blazed from his blue eyes.

"You were?" she said softly, achingly.

"Yes, I was."

"Oh." Lily stared at him, helplessly mesmerized by the handsome face bent to hers, lit with tenderness and a passion that she craved.

Trace's fingers tightened over hers where they rested on his sleeve.

"We're getting out of here," he said huskily, and kept her fingers covered with his when he turned back to his father and great-uncle.

"Trace," Gavin said. "This is your cousin, Nicholas. Nick, this is my son, Trace, and his friend, Lily Townsend."

Somehow, Trace and Lily managed to get through the introductions and the necessary few moments of polite conversation before they could gracefully leave.

Nicholas watched them walk away, blue eyes speculative.

"I think you're going to have another wedding to go to, Uncle Nathan," he observed with a small male grin of appreciation.

"I wouldn't doubt it." Nathan's keen gaze fastened approvingly on the couple exiting the Lakeshore before catching sight of a familiar red-gold crown of hair near at hand. "There's someone I want you to meet, Nicholas. Kari," he called, crooking a finger at Meg Stewart's daughter. "Come here."

Nick's gaze sharpened as the redhead turned, her face lighting with a smile that turned her face from pretty to beautiful.

Nathan's sharp gaze didn't miss the interest on Nick's face and he smiled complacently.

"I thought I was never going to get you alone," Trace groaned, nibbling Lily's ear while he fumbled with her zipper. "I love my sister, but this wedding was rotten timing. I don't feel like sharing you with several hundred people."

Lily laughed softly and tipped her head sideways to allow him better access to the soft skin of her throat. Her own fingers were busy with his shirt buttons.

Trace growled with satisfaction as the stubborn zipper gave way and he could peel the dress away from her skin. He pushed it down over her hips and leaned away from her to look down at her.

"Damn," he breathed, his hot gaze sizzling as it ran over the pink merry widow that lifted full breasts and cinched in an already tiny waist above brief pink lace bikini panties. "If I'd known you were wearing these, I never would have made it through the ceremony!"

"Really?" Lily loved his unreserved admiration. It bolstered her self-esteem and melted her bones. "You make me feel sexy," she whispered.

"Good," he growled. "Show me."

He picked her up and dropped onto the bed with her.

It was a long time later before they lay propped up against the bed pillows and the headboard, temporarily sated.

Trace cradled her body against his, the black silk of her hair tickling his chin. He wasn't sure she was ready to accept him, but he'd waited as long as he could.

"Lily . . ." he began. "I want you to move in with me."

"Move in with you?" she repeated cautiously. Living together was not what she wanted. She wanted marriage.

Trace heard the doubt in her voice and his arms tightened unconsciously around her, as if to banish any possibilty of refusal.

"Yes." This time his voice held unrelenting, won't-take-no determination. "I'm not sleeping without you again. As far as I'm concerned, we said our vows today in front of that altar and we're already married. But until we can do it legally, you're staying here."

Stunned, Lily tipped her head back to look up at him. His jaw was set aggressively and his blue gaze held a militant sheen.

"All right," she said calmly.

"All right?" His face reflected surprise, shock, and then pure delight. "No arguments? No lectures about my making macho demands?"

"Nope." She smiled, that same sweet curving of her lips that had sent him tumbling head-over-heels in love with her at first meeting. "Why would I argue? You just gave me everything I've ever wanted; when Pastor Larson was speaking today, I knew that I want and need exactly what you told me you wanted, your Sunday kind of love, forever and ever, amen."

"Dad and Mom are going to be in seventh heaven," he said. "Especially if we give them grandchildren." A gleam sparked his blue eyes. "You know, if we really try, I bet we could have a baby before Jesse and Sarah."

"Having children is *not* a contest," Lily admonished, eyeing him severely.

"No, but *trying* to have them is a lot of fun," he said huskily, blue eyes twinkling.

"You're right," she sighed as he buried his face against her throat and began to nibble at her ear again. *He's always been right about that*, she thought. *He really is a lot of fun.* And then she lost the ability to think as his mouth moved lower.

No. 17 OPENING ACT by Ann Patrick
Big city playwright meets small town sheriff and life heats up.

No. 18 RAINBOW WISHES by Jacqueline Case
Mason is looking for more from life. Evie may be his pot of gold!

No. 19 SUNDAY DRIVER by Valerie Kane
Carrie breaks through all Cam's defenses showing him how to love.

No. 20 CHEATED HEARTS by Karen Lawton Barrett
T.C. and Lucas find their way back into each other's hearts.

No. 22 NEVER LET GO by Laura Phillips
Ryan has a big dilemma. Kelly is the answer to *all* his prayers.

No. 23 A PERFECT MATCH by Susan Combs
Ross can keep Emily safe but can he save himself from Emily?

No. 24 REMEMBER MY LOVE by Pamela Macaluso
Will Max ever remember the special love he and Deanna shared?

---

**Kismet Romances**
Dept. 1291, P. O. Box 41820, Philadelphia, PA 19101-9828

Please send the books I've indicated below. Check or money order only—no cash, stamps or C.O.D.s (PA residents, add 6% sales tax). I am enclosing $2.95 plus 75¢ handling fee for *each* book ordered.
**Total Amount Enclosed: $__________.**

| | | | |
|---|---|---|---|
| ___ No. 4 | ___ No. 6 | ___ No. 12 | ___ No. 18 |
| ___ No. 21 | ___ No. 7 | ___ No. 13 | ___ No. 19 |
| ___ No. 1 | ___ No. 8 | ___ No. 14 | ___ No. 20 |
| ___ No. 2 | ___ No. 9 | ___ No. 15 | ___ No. 22 |
| ___ No. 3 | ___ No. 10 | ___ No. 16 | ___ No. 23 |
| ___ No. 5 | ___ No. 11 | ___ No. 17 | ___ No. 24 |

*Please Print:*
Name ______________________________
Address ____________________ Apt. No. ________
City/State ____________________ Zip ________

Allow four to six weeks for delivery. Quantities limited.